# REDSINE TEN

OCTOBER 2002

EDITED BY
**TRENT JAMIESON** AND **GARRY NURRISH**

REDSINE
a quarterly magazine of dark fantasy & horror

ISBN: 1-894815-03-3

Published by Prime Books, Inc.
P.O. Box 36503, Canton, OH 44735, USA
www.primebooks.net



For more information, contact Redsine.

Acknowledgments:
"When Fire Knew My Name" by James Sallis previously published in *Fantastic Metropolis* website, 2001.

Redsine editors:
Garry Nurrish, Senior Editor—garry@redsine.com
Trent Jamieson, Fiction Editor—trent@redsine.com
Nick Gevers, Interviewer—nickgevers@redsine.com

REDSINE MAGAZINE
PO Box 1287, Toowong, QLD 4066, Australia
www.redsine.com

# CONTENTS



FOR AUTHOR BIOGRAPHIES, PLEASE VISIT THE
REDSINE WEBSITE AT: www.redsine.com/10bios.html

# WHEN FIRE KNEW MY NAME

## BY JAMES SALLIS

Cold, driving weather like this always brought them out.

It had been there in early morning, a presence, a threat, a promise, and by seven had honed itself to a cleaver-like edge on the strop of wind. From my window on the fifth floor I listened to the schlep-schlep-schlep of that edge on the strop and watched as day congealed and the blade began to slice away at the city.

They emerged on their canes and crutches, in wheelchairs, tottering on artificial and makeshift limbs or balanced like flat-bottomed urns on low carts, pulling themselves along with gloved hands. At these times there is an expression on their faces that's difficult to describe. Pain, yes—but within it, at the core, the thing that pain comes wrapped around, a kind of joyfulness, I think.

Others, those to whom the world belonged, walked with heads down, swaddled in scarves and layers of wool and heavy caps. But the survivors tore open their own shabby coats and raised faces to the sky, threw out their arms to embrace it all: this wind, this blade, this impossible city.

"Don't tell me. The fire brigade's out." Somehow or another, originating in the punch line of a joke, I'm sure, that had become our name for them. Sandra stood in the doorway arch whose frame evoked both Chinese calligraphy and pi with sheet and blanket wrapped about her, a human teepee. Her hair, so blond it was almost white, had begun growing back in. It poked out a quarter-inch or so all around and she was convinced she looked like a dandelion. "Shut the shockin' window before your nose falls off."

"Yeah, and I've only got *one* of those."

In college, as was the fad for a couple of years, she'd had an ear removed. Half the people in the city her age were walking around with newly grown ones, but that wasn't Sandra's style. She started something, she stayed with it.

"If I shut the window, it frosts over and I can't see out."

"What—they look different this time?"

But of course they never did. They were as generic and predictable as spring, as the run of our daily lives, the news and entertainment piped in to us, what we said to one another. I shut the window. Wind howled as though in complaint and shook the pane fiercely with both hands.

"Breakfast?"

"I'd planned on fishes, but we're fresh out of loaves."

"The cupboard was bare."

"In a word."

"Not even a bone."

"A few exoskeletons, but I don't think those count."

Sandra and wrappings sank into one of the chairs. "I was dreaming," she told me. "Standing on the street looking up at a billboard." With one hand she sketched its cadence, form and line breaks on air. "We're almost done/ World finished soon/ Thank you for your patience/ B&D Construction.

"I'm standing there and I have this warm feeling in my stomach. I realise that for months, as cold winds blew in across bare plains to the east, I've been coming out each morning to admire new buildings that appear overnight, to be among the first to stroll new plazas, arcades, explore tiny parks. I'm tremendously proud of my city, what it's becoming.

"But there's also, it seems, a problem. When I return to my apartment, six brutally handsome young men in jeans, black T-shirts and low-slung toolbelts are waiting in the hall outside. They have to tear out my floor, they say. Possibly the walls as well. They'll know once they get started. But will I be able to stay here while you work? I ask them. Sure, no problem, the foreman says. Long as you don't need a floor or walls."

Rising, Sandra walked into the kitchen area and, ever the child of

Famine parents, came out with a half-loaf of bread fetched from one hiding spot or another. I drew hot water, crumbled in tea leaves, and we fell to.

We'd been together almost four years. I'd gone with friends to HOUSE OF th'OUGHT and wound up sitting beside her. The House was another of those intermittent hot spots thronged with patrons for months when it opened, afterwards all but abandoned. Here great books were read aloud, in shifts, by professional readers. We were never able to agree on what was being read at the time. I remembered *Tristram Shandy*; Sandra insisted that by then Burning Cinder Person, the House's star reader and frequent subject of profiles in local papers during the House's brief heyday, was well into the 19th century.

(*In halflight she turns, murmuring, and I trace the scars along her back, by the shoulder blades. The sky splits open like a wound, and birds cough the sun into morning.*)

"So what's on for today?" she asked.

"Have to deliver my Cowboy tapes to Epoch-Z."

Cowboy's a figure so legendary that many claim he never existed. Supposedly he was the first of the great urban freedom fighters—some say the last as well—and went down in the siege of the markets. But street wisdom has it that Cowboy's still out there. He'd never been photographed except—possibly—for less than sixty seconds of blurry footage I'd caught years ago while filming deconstruction of the Skystop Building. One of the news channels was putting together a documentary on Cowboy. They'd learned of my tapes and offered enough money to keep me afloat, us afloat, for a year.

"What, you can't just shoot it to them? You're going outside? To someone's shockin' office?"

I shrugged. "They actually called up, on the phone. 'We may be on the bitter sharp edge, but we're also a little old-fashioned 'round here,' they tell me, 'in our own way.' Before I know it, I'm in a conference call with half a dozen vice presidents ranging in age between eighteen and eighteen-and-a-half. 'We like our people to have faces,' they tell me."

Jack London said to understand totalitarianism, picture a boot heel stamping on a human face—forever. Big business is soft Italian-leather loafers caressing that same face. However long and hard we espouse bohemian, alternative, libertarian, contrary lifestyles, we all live off big business, fleas on a dog. I tried to remember when heads of major corporations had begun showing up for work in pullovers and jeans. Revolution in America? Radical change? The country's very genius is its capacity to absorb anything, absolutely *anything*—to appropriate it, bear it on a flood into the mainstream, vitiate it.

"Anything I can pick up while I'm out?" I asked.

"Ginger would be good, for tonight's curry. Oh, and I guess some vegetables and rice. So there'll *be* a curry? Assuming I ever see you again."

"Think of it as an adventure," I said.

"Think of it as stupid," she said. "Not to mention the possibility of freezing nose, fingers and like wee appendages off."

"*Wee?* Did you say *wee?*" Reaching for a Scottish accent, which came out, inexplicably, Jamaican.

"Don't forget the ginger."

We say it together: "A Redemptionist never forgets."

*

There on the street away from river's edge, I encountered a more normal population—normal for this quarter of the city, that is. Fully half those out in the bite and slash hobbled along on feet with tendons fatally damaged by the police's standard interrogation technique: if they didn't like your answer, they stood on your foot and heaved you mightily backwards. Meanwhile uptown folk were paying clinics huge sums to have facial muscles injected with botulism. The bacteria paralyse the muscle and, in doing so, erase age lines. When these people talk, their eyebrows don't move but float cloudlike above their mouths, like dialogue balloons in cartoons.

I began to penetrate the city's many folds and strata. I've always suspected it to be more laminate than veneer, thin sheets pressed close to form something of apparent substance, nothing, not even inferior materials, at its core.

At the corner of Market and Force, several hundred protesters converged in absolute silence on the plaza before City Hall. Riot police formed a human moat around the complex, beating sticks backhand against shields. The juxtaposition was uncanny. Protesters stood motionless looking across. Police beat at their shields. At some invisible cue the protesters withdrew as silently as they'd come.

At First and Desire, a small park had been set fire by the Children's Army. *We burn the bones they throw us,* a placard read. Children in red armbands stood alongside monitoring, making certain the fires did not spread. The fires were doing anything but, however. They were lowering, folding in upon themselves, benches turning to smoulder. One of the children stepped forward into the park and gave a fingers-into-palm, come-to-me sign. *Incoming,* he shouted as half a dozen Molotov cocktails rained from windows of the high-rise project skirting the park.

Two blocks up, a crowd had gathered. They shouted encouragement, chanted, raised fists in the air. Leaning against the wall of a nearby credit union was a piece of cardboard cut from a heavy box and laboriously hand-lettered in cockeyed, backward-leaning block letters.

STREET FITING!

It was already over, though, the crowd dispersing, as I approached. One man lay broken and bleeding, body in the street, head on the curb as though on a pillow. I watched as his eyes went still. The other, the winner, wiped blood from his eyes and picked up the hat with the money. Then he walked to the sign, lifted it for a closer look, tucked it underarm. His now. Spoils.

The city I find when I come out into it, the one I'm a part of, is invisible to many. As though the city's gone belly up, as though this grey sky were an overturned stone. These are the forgotten people, the ones who don't matter, those ground down on the city's mill, used up, thrown beneath the wheels. Here there is neither history nor future, only a perpetual present tense of motion, hunger, need and momentary ease, a fire that consumes and goes on consuming, through whose flickering silent tongues sometimes we glimpse the shape, the form, the suggestion, of another reality, another world. A better one? Different, at least. And different is enough.

"Cowboy!" I cried out.

He stood at a street corner, buckskin fringe blowing in the breeze, looking a little confused when I approached him. We were at the dangerous border between uptown and down. Age lines crouched like homesteaders, deepset, at eyes and mouth. I took note of the missing ear.

"What's up?" I said. Like so many others, looking for guidance.

"What's ever up but more of the same? Just they practice new grimaces in the mirror is all, tell us more outrageous lies. You feel connected?"

No.

But had I ever?

"We have to keep changing. Dodging under, going over, scrambling. We can't let them get a hold, take us for granted."

"But you . . . "

Seeing the sudden sadness in his eyes, I understood. He was an icon. He couldn't change.

"Here's my ride," he said, stepping not into the city bus one would have thought he awaited but into an ancient VW bus. "Keep the faith?"

I watched him pull away.

Against the horizon the day still burned into life and burned steadily away, like alcohol, in a blue flame. No heat to any of it. What could a man do?

After a moment I snapped an earplug off the tab and fit it in as I started walking again along the street, past crews of workers tearing up streets, crews of workers rebuilding them. You never know what you'll get, of course, that's part of the deal, but this was okay. *We'll Meet Again in Glory.* I watched my breath go out in plumes with each step.

Glory was the next town over.

# RED ON RED

## BY JENNIFER WHITE

On the side of the track the eucalypts tremble. They are the earth's antennae, listening for something we cannot hear. The tops of the trees shiver delicately, sprinkling a permanent patina of red dust over everything. She is covered in it. It sticks to her like red Xmas glitter. She pushes brusquely past the trees, stamping along the track with her spade-like feet, her fat toes gripping the rubber thongs she wears, kicking the dirt up and back onto herself. She's relaxed. She doesn't care what she looks like. Who can see her here? Her plump middle flops over the waistband of her shorts.

Funny how in such a large, empty land there are crowds everywhere. People following her. Chasing her so that they can watch her big tits wobble. And she laughs, too, breathless and embarrassed. It's the only attention she ever gets.

But right now she's alone, and in order to celebrate that fact she sings. It's a throaty, tuneless sound, or perhaps it's a tune with different rules, different times. No matter. She sings for herself. To give herself pleasure. She relishes the thrum at the back of her throat. She can't get enough of it. She rolls the air around in her mouth like a boiled lolly, collecting spit, and pushes out the sound, thin and bubbling into the vast amphitheatre she has chosen.

"You're asking for trouble," her mother said. "Everyone knows you do it, go bush. And anyway, you're nearly a grown woman. You should be staying closer to home. You're getting to that dangerous time when anything might happen."

Someone did follow her once, a kid from school. "Yah," he called, his voice high and strangled and thick with snot. He came up fast behind her and stood there with his fists at his waist, legs wide apart. "Yer no good," he screamed. "Yer a slut. Yer askin' for it." If it hadn't been so hurtful she would have laughed. She, such a great ugly lump of a girl, asking for it? She could have died laughing.

He stood there, maroon-faced, opening his mouth wide to shout some more, baring his yellow teeth.

But he forgot, because all he saw before him was girl, that she was bigger than him. She turned, it was like some vast stone monument turning slowly, purposefully, and she began to run towards him with those heavy, stiff, log-like legs. He ran, too, but she caught him easily. He stood there, panting, staring at her, waiting to see what she would do. He wiped the snot from his nose with the back of his hand. She pushed him down on the dirt and put a foot on his back. "I can see up yer shorts," he sneered.

Back at school he yelled whenever he saw her. "Yer loved it. Yer know yer did." His mates cackled with glee. She stood there mute, with her impassive Easter Island stare, containing the pain.

And now, alone in the bush, when she sang her strange passion she always wondered if someone was following, listening.

That's what she thought it was that last time, when she crept out of the house, away from her mum's constant supervision, away from the rowdy good cheer of her six siblings. She was being followed, she knew it. How? Oh, by the density of the air around her, perhaps. Or the staccato flurry of birds' wings overhead. But, because of it she denied herself the pleasure of singing. Three times she stopped and waited for whomever it was to show themselves. The third time she was determined. She squatted there in the red dust and waited for an hour. Two hours. She panted slightly from nerves and because it was a hot, dry day.

And whoever it was watched her all that time.

After two hours a pale, heavy-jowled dog pushed through the undergrowth to meet her. It sat before her, cocked its head to one side, and smiled revealing powerful fangs. She could smell its breath.

"You stink," she laughed with relief.

It lifted one paw like a trained dog, a Hollywood Rin Tin Tin of a dog, and this appealed to her, even if it was artificial and manipulative. She thought it was cute. The dog stood and walked ahead a little, then stopped and turned to look at her as if to say, "Well, what are you waiting for?"

It wants me to follow, she thought, and it felt so nice to be wanted for anything that she forgot to ask herself why the dog had been stalking her, why it had watched her from the undergrowth for two hours. She followed, smiling all the while at the dog's cleverness and at her own willingness to do what it said. What have I got to lose after all, she shrugged. She enjoyed the delicate softness of the animal's tread, the soft, rhythmic padding of its four paws in the dirt. She followed the sound more than anything.

It was afternoon now, and hotter than ever. The sweat dribbled down her back and into her pink bike shorts and the crack of her arse. By late afternoon she had changed her mind. Now she thought it was silly. They were going nowhere, just further and further into the centre. "I'm going back dog," she called.

The animal turned and snarled a warning. It was telling her that she had left it too late. She had come this far, she couldn't turn back. She realised suddenly that she had been following a wild beast.

She laughed a little, pretended still that it was just a game, and animal and girl continued on. She told herself that she could stop anytime. She was, after all, a human girl with certain powers of reason and intellect. He was only a dog. But they had already come such a long way, and she was drying out in the heat. She was a husk. Only the essence of her was left, the essential elements.

The shadows lengthened. The girl stopped. Even if she returned now it would still be the middle of the night by the time she reached home. She backed quietly away from the dog, intending to turn and run. But how could she have ever thought that her clumsy tread would be softer than this animal's? It knew instantly what she was up to and it sprang upon her.

It caught her by surprise. Otherwise she would have fought, pushed at his fangs, poked at his eyes. She knew how to fight. His teeth burst a major artery before she could even sort out in her tired brain what was happening. The blood pumped out of her in rhythmic spurts all over the Nirvana T-shirt she wore. Chunks of gore slid down her arm. He had ripped a huge hole in her. She could feel strips of skin flapping open, and the air, cold now, on her torn flesh. She could see the cold yellow eyes of the beast. He sat beside her, watching, waiting.

And then she was in eclipse.

When she woke she felt the ground moving beneath her. The beast was dragging her by her right foot, so delicately that she could hardly feel it. But she could feel her throat. Dust choked the wound, irritating and scraping at its rawness. Blood still dripped out of her and onto the earth. Red on red. It was a wonder she had any blood left. And the pain, it was so large that it was completely beyond her. She hadn't caught up with it yet, but she would.

Next thing, she was in a place between two rocks, a dark place, a cool place. It was like being in the shallows of the ocean, like a rock pool, only instead of water rippling around her, it was light reflecting and shimmering off shiny rocks. She was panting for water, or for air, she was not sure which. She sensed that she had been there already for a long time, days perhaps. She felt the pain now. She was turning inside out with it. Her skin was raw, new, it felt like it had been rubbed all over in sand. It went on for hours. The beast—she'd thought he was a dog but now she saw that she had been wrong— brought her small animals every so often, ripped in half. He offered their bodies up to her like bowls of chicken soup. He shoved them at her. She was thirsty. She lapped at the congealing blood.

"Oooh, oooh." He laughed as he watched her. "There, that's better," he said.

Surprisingly soon she was ready to stand, though the first time she tried, her legs felt like matchsticks from lying down for so long. Her clothes were gone. It took her a while to get used to being naked. At first she dug under the sand to cover herself. She shivered, even though it was hot, at the thought of such complete exposure, and she spent a whole morning looking for her T-shirt. But a new power threaded through her and made her forget about stupid things like clothes. She had the strength now of something that had become other than what it was born. Her golden fur, flat at first and covered with a type of clear, gelid substance, glistened in the sun. She ran to see what running was like with four legs instead of two. The beast himself allowed her to wrestle with him, so that she could test herself. The muscles moved under her skin like small, lively animals. It was the first time she had ever enjoyed having a body.

She was grateful. She had wanted things to be different.

The beast taught her how to hunt and what the smells meant. He was wise, she could see it in the cast of his eyes. And if there was a certain smugness in the way he conducted himself, well, it was something she could forgive.

"That spicy stink," she said. "Like rotten meat dressed with exotic herbs. What is it?"

"They're the ghosts," he told her. "The flat-faced ones, the pearl-skins. They are what you used to be."

She didn't ask what she was now.

Did her family know she was gone? she wondered. Did her mother realise that she had not returned. Did her brothers and sisters notice that there was one less of them? She suspected that any small space in the house due to her absence would have closed up almost immediately, like flesh cut cleanly, and left no sign of anything amiss. Her mother had warned her that something would happen to her if she kept going bush. Is this what she had meant?

They got along well enough, the two of them, the beast and she, until she attacked him one day. She made up reasons for it, like resentment, like she hadn't chosen this life. You can always find an excuse to fight. But, really, it was because she knew she could do it and get away with it. She had always been powerful and had always held herself back. Now she didn't have to any more, not even against him.

And that was all.

She had to prove it, test it. She brought him down and wounded him, and in her terror she fled. Weeks later she returned, but his smell was gone.

Without the beast she was utterly alone. But she was, by nature, and by inclination, a solitary being so she enjoyed it well enough, or at least it didn't send her half mad as it would have some. And if she needed company the dingoes let her sing with them of a night, though not too close, mind. She might have looked like them, but they could easily smell her difference. When she came near they backed away slowly and carefully. Their hair stood erect at the thought of her and of her kind. They thought she might jump them and eat their flesh, and she might have, too, if she were hungry or in the mood.

And that other, first life, that soft white larval stage of a life, moved further and further away. Sometimes, though, she dreamed of it and woke afterwards with a deep unease, for there was still something of that other, social creature in her. But it passed soon enough. She always felt better after she killed.

At times like these she haunted the edges of the human camps. She remembered their scents and their songs. They left a trail of smells wherever they went. The earth was criss-crossed with them like old scars never quite fading. She was drawn to them but she was appropriately cautious for she knew that, very often, you are drawn to that which can hurt you the most.

The smells were sweet and dark to her. Irresistible. She didn't hunt them, though, the humans. She knew that if you hurt one of them, you hurt the whole pack. They were too much trouble. She remembered that much. But she ate their companions, the dogs. The dogs smelled better anyway.

And every day she remembered less. Eventually there would only be the now, the continuous now. She would forget what a day was. She would forget that the sun would set until it did. Even now it surprised her and pleased her to see a fine sunset. And then to see the glittering stones far above her in the velvet dark.

That's what she was doing at the campsite that night. Bathing in its warmth, craving its painful comfort for reasons she had almost forgotten. Her nose twitched at the smells. She could hear high hooting sounds that had to be laughter, and the tinkling of bottles and cans, and she could hear car doors open and shut, and engines rev. And then she was on her belly, crawling nearer, dangerously near, for if they saw her, if they sensed what she really was, and how could they not with just one look into her beastly eyes, they would destroy her.

She was a mystery, and mystery must be contained.

She crawled closer, flattening grass, rustling past trees, her powerful muscled limbs pulling her closer and closer until someone came her way, almost treading on her. He wanted a piss. She ducked quickly into a shelter that was a little removed from the others, meaning only to hide herself until they passed. She stood there waiting and listening. It was dark, and in the gloom she could see a pattern of ordinary, everyday objects made sinister by the darkness and by her own faulty memory of their purpose. There were suitcases and a lamp, a folding chair and a low cot, and in the cot a young one. The young one was not crying, just playing with the ribbon on its woollen jacket. It was a very little one, so easy for her to carry, and she hadn't known what she was going to do until she was already slipping through the opening of the shelter and running from the camp with the baby in her mouth. The baby did not cry.

She tried to be gentle, but the act had to be savage. There had to be risk. There was blood, of course, mingled with saliva, and the baby's eyes turned blank like windblown fruit that's been pecked at by birds, but she brought the little one a fresh kill, just as one had been brought for her, and pushed it up to the little one's face. And the child sucked up the blood, her tiny pink tongue lapping, and her lids fluttering, and smiling up at her.

# McKENDRICK'S BAYONET

## BY FORREST AGUIRRE & SCOTT THOMAS

The gunfire ringing in Sergeant William McKendrick's ears melted into the buzz of mosquito and tsetse. The harsh taste of cordite gave way to salty sweat, though powder smoke still clouded the air around the handful of khaki-dressed troops as they regrouped. McKendrick felt ill at ease about the lull. He knew the Bembele would return, and with over half his men gone and all direction lost, he would have a difficult time leading his troops home through the jungle. Up here, behind the ur-wall of an ancient stone fortress, they might hold out indefinitely. All approaches were covered by his best surviving marksmen and a solid supply of ammunition boxes had been saved before the quartermaster's coach had been over run by the assegai-weilding natives.

No such supply of ration boxes, however, could be rescued before the quartermaster and his men were skewered through by the onslaught of ebony warriors. Food would run out the next day and the roads that thrust out from the revetment's base like tropical jellyfish tendrils into the green hell gave little hope for a rendezvous with any remaining troop bodies; if any troops out there were left alive after the rout. The last echoes of gunshots had echoed off into the night at least half an hour ago. This did not bode well. If he survived, McKendrick would spend a great deal of time penning letters of condolence to wives and mothers, brothers and sons.

A hippopotamus calf, caught in the crossfire of their last firefight, lay dead on the jungle floor. The Sergeant ordered the animal skinned and a bonfire built; strange orders that came to sense only after McKendrick constructed a miniature zeppelin out of the hide, filling it with hot air from the fire. Private Hammish, a young redheaded lad known for his keen eyesight, was strapped to the contraption and raised through the rainforest ceiling as a lookout. At least it was cooler up top, his companions joked, where the upper canopy of trees released its sticky humidity into the free night air.

"Well? What do you make out," McKendrick yelled.

"Full moon. No fires. Only movement is the breeze and some birds, maybe bats."

"Sir, maybe they left," Dermit, another Private.

"Not bloody likely. Corporal Duncan, what does our scout think?"

The two-striped Scotsman turned to his jet-black compatriot: "Natatu?"

The askari, dressed in colonial khaki as his white peers, but sans the black kilt of the Black Watch, spewed off a string of syllables only intelligible to the Corporal.

"Kwa Sababu?" Duncan asked.

Another flood of words and a nod.

"Says you're right, sir. They'll be back, after they free the souls of the dead."

"Ignorant bastards," McKendrick smiled and shook his head. "So they have to drum up the ghosts, then?"

"No, sir. Cut them out."

"What?"

"Cut them out, sir. The Bembele believe that a brave warrior's soul can only be free after the body is disembowelled, thus putting the spirit at liberty to visit its family one last time before ascending to heaven."

The smile faded from the Sergeant's face even as a grin spread across the face of the askari. McKendrick shook his head in disgust. "And what happens if the soul stays in the body?"

The askari's countenance went slack. "Baya sana! Evil! No good!"

"The spirit becomes malignant, sir," Duncan explained, "prone to control by sorcerers who consume human flesh. This is why a warrior must always fight bravely, so his enemy will free his soul out of respect for the fallen hero."

"Sir, something approaching!" Private Hammish called down. Rifle bolts clicked almost in unison.

McKendrick half shouted, half whispered up: "What is it, son?"

A few tense moments of mosquito-buzzing near-silence, then: "False alarm," from above. "Just a few giraffes walking up a pathway. They'll be near us soon."

The askari bolted up to his feet: "Giraffe? Hapana! No!"

Their heads bobbed through the trees, the animals' chests level with the fortress walls just as the pith-helmeted black wheeled to fire at the animals. The men sat stunned as the upper pelts, necks and heads dropped to the ground, revealing the animate corpses of their fallen comrades, giraffe legs strapped to their supernaturally-mobile limbs like stilts. A void malignance glowered dark in their empty eye sockets as they abandoned their grim prostheses and swarmed over the fortress wall, their bloated corpses flowering red blossoms as their erstwhile companions blasted holes into their distended bellies. Privates Carlisle, McDivet, Dickinson, Brucely, Williamson and the quartermaster, Flannigan, groped and bludgeoned their way through the shock-stiffened bodies of their fellow soldiers, low raspy moans escaping from their hideous, toothless maws—each rictus shrivelled in eternal mummification. Only the askari, who gutted the nearest attacker—Flannigan—with his bayonet, was not immediately over-whelmed but he soon succumbed to the flailing arms of death.

McKendrick fell back over the outside wall and down a steep slope as his scout was pummelled to death by his allies-in-life. Hammish screamed and kicked from above as the undead soldiers dragged him down, helpless, from his aerie. The last thing the Sergeant saw by the flickering firelight was the group of animate dead feasting on the limbs of their countrymen, tearing off bits of flesh and stuffing them past their bloodied gums. In the distance behind him, a drumbeat boomed through the forest, reverberating against its green roof. His ankle sprained, fingers broken from the fall, McKendrick hobbled off into the jungle night.

*

The last echoes of gunshots had echoed off into the night at least half an hour ago. Major William McKendrick climbed up out of a muddy trench into the damp French air. It was dark—the flares no longer fizzling above like shredded moons, the canon shells now at rest, like chrysalides of flame.

In the murk and the stench, beneath a mist of lingering smoke, there appeared bodies. No groans, no moans, no movement, only bodies. McKendrick unshouldered his Lee Enfield. The mud made kissing sounds each time he lifted a boot.

McKendrick stopped to inspect one of the bodies, rolling it onto its back with his foot. The damp air ached in his fingers, twenty-two years since they were broken, and still they ached. He looked down dispassionately at the dead blond Bosch then moved along.

Wet footsteps behind him, but not the dead, this time.

"Major . . ."

McKendrick affixed a long thin bayonet to the end of his rifle.

"Major, wait . . ."

McKendrick walked on, stopped, stooped over a figure. The hair and most of the face were missing, but the uniform was British.

Sergeant Murphy caught up, panting and started to say, "Sir, 'tain't safe—might be snipers—"

McKendrick pointed his rifle down and jammed the bayonet into the abdomen of his broken comrade.

"Jesus, Major! He's one of us!" the sergeant gasped.

"I know," McKendrick said, tugging the blade from side to side until the dead man's bowels slid free.

*

The last echoes of gunshots had echoed off into the Somerset night at least half an hour ago. The servants reappeared slowly, cautiously, peering around this and that corner as they did each time the master indulged in one of his shooting binges. Major William McKendrick was slumped in his leather chair in the shadow-stained study, a near-empty bottle tipped and dripping silently onto the rug.

There had never been a Mrs McKendrick, nor any little McKendricks. The major was married to his memories. He dreamed them now, the Lee Enfield spent, across his legs, his arthritic hands twitching like pale birds in the dark.

Of course it was only the wind, he thought, stirring. He barely heard the figure entering the study. He grinned through his beard, half chuckling, half coughing.

"Good evening," McKendrick said

"Good evening, Sir. Are you quite well, Sir?" It was the manservant Holloway, portly and balding and calm. He bent and gently lifted his master's rifle, moving it to a dim corner.

"Shall I light the fire, Sir?"

"Don't bother, Mr Holloway," McKendrick sighed.

"Shall I see you up to bed then?" McKendrick studied his servant, loyal these ten years since the Great War.

"Tell me," the master said, sitting up in his Negro-coloured chair, "have you ever seen them?"

Impassive, without veering from his monotone, Holloway responded, "Them, Sir?"

"The dead. Surely . . . "

"I'm afraid not, Sir." It was the same answer he had been giving for ten years now.

McKendrick drew a deep breath and wagged his head, turned his face toward the window.

"Did I not shoot anything in the garden tonight?"

Holloway cleared his throat.

"A crow, Sir."

McKendrick half-remembered a dead crow placed on a stone garden bench, a penknife sinking into its belly, feathers fluttering down like black petals.

"Ahh, yes, only a crow. Well, well. Mr Holloway, would you be so kind as to fetch me that paper there on my desk?"

Holloway swivelled away, went to the desk. McKendrick spoke to the man's back. "I'll be wanting my rifle as well. The paper is a contract I've written up, Mr Holloway. Read it and sign it and my house and land will be yours."

His back to his master, Holloway read the words, the letters like the shadow of mandrake roots. He let it drop back onto the desk and turned.

"Sir . . . "

"Think me mad if you must, Holloway, but sign the bloody

thing."

McKendrick was growing impatient.

"I cannot do this, Sir." Holloway actually had a touch of emotion in his voice.

"You'll be a wealthy man, Holloway; all you need do is open me up."

Holloway, without another word, went briskly to the rifle, grabbed it from the corner and headed for the door. Calling to the butler's back, McKendrick said, "You should see their mouths, Holloway—their horrible toothless mouths!"

Holloway closed the door and locked it from the outside and was set to rush off for the village to fetch Dr Hemmings when he heard the shot. He had forgotten about the Webley-Fosbery revolver in Major McKendrick's desk.

Holloway unlocked the study and found McKendrick by his desk, face up, staring, splashes of blood like red wings expanding from his head.

"Dear God!" Holloway knelt by the body and placed his hand on the chest. He felt nothing. Closer, he put his ear to the body. He heard the wind outside, a whisper at the window and soft ticking sounds. Sleet? The wind with cats of ice at the glass. No heartbeat. Holloway sat up and stared at the blood, a flattened headdress of red, still spreading.

Now there was hail at the window, insistent and loud, the nails of ten thousand bony fingers. High tea came rushing up in his throat and he dashed to the window, opened it. The contents of Holloway's stomach went out and small white pelting objects rained in. Teeth. Tens of thousands of teeth from the clear night sky. Teeth like dice skipping over the study floor, skidding like bits of porcelain, teeth in the garden, winking into the birdbath, clattering on the roof, falling on the McKendrick property and nowhere else.

Holloway finished retching, closed the window and collected himself. He gazed down at the Major for a moment, then crossed the room toward a windowed cabinet to fetch the bayonet that lay rusting among dusty medals.

# RAKE AT THE GATES OF HELL

## BY DIRK FLINTHEART

Severed by a wall of jagged obsidian, the plain stretched into the shimmering distance. On either side of the wall, the ground looked the same; a baking hot expanse of shards and pebbles, without so much as a hill or a tree to break the monotony. ScabRat, however, propped against his pitchfork of black iron, knew that there was one extremely important difference. Easing his position atop the wall, ScabRat was painfully aware that one side of the wall was Hell. The other was not. Of course, during the long tours of guard duty on the lonely reaches, it wasn't always easy to remember which was which.

A faint sound came from somewhere over ScabRat's shoulder. *Bless me,* he thought angrily. *I'm all turned about again!*

He turned and raised his trident, wishing yet again that the Powers would just once forget to keep the metal painfully hot. Still, thought ScabRat, *it's Hell, after all. It could be worse. I could be a damned soul in the lake of boiling blood.* The sound came again, and he looked for the source. Not far away, shambling over the stones, he saw a naked man. His eyes were fixed on the wall, and with the grim determination known only to the Damned, he advanced.

"Ahem," said ScabRat. His voice sounded strange and creaky. How many decades had it been since the last escapee? "Was there something you wanted?"

The man looked up at ScabRat, who studied him in turn. Somewhere in his early forties, ScabRat judged, with a powerful physique and an unusual collection of scars.

The man put his hands on his hips. "I'd be grateful for a hand up yon wall," he said, in an accent that spoke of lush peat bogs, and good whiskey. "Unless ye know a handy gate. I've come a mortal long way, and I don't mind telling ye, I'm sore tired." He mopped his face. "I'm not the man I was, and that's the truth."

ScabRat grinned lazily. "Of course I'll help you, friend," he oozed, extending his fork. "Just grab on and I'll pull you up. Then we can have a nice, long chat, eh?"

The man eyed the fork a moment. "Kind of you," he said.

ScabRat waited with a certain inner glee for the scream as the fool closed his fingers over the blistering-hot prongs of the iron fork, but he was disappointed. The man frowned, readjusting his grip. "Bugger me," he swore, (ScabRat made a mental note to grant his request at the first opportunity) "That's a bit hot, eh?" Nevertheless, he grasped the tines firmly, and tugged.

ScabRat, poised on his haunches with the heavy fork extended full length, was caught unawares. The sudden jerk overbalanced him, and he plummeted heavily onto his back amongst the bitterly sharp stones.

"Sorry about that," said the man cheerfully. He extended a hand which ScabRat ignored. "Now we're both stuck out here, eh?"

"Fool!" growled ScabRat, heaving himself to his feet. A stabbing pain shot through his kidneys. "You will pay for this."

The man grinned through his patchy brown beard. "It's eternity. What's another punishment or two? Now, are yis going to help us up that wall?"

They stared at the glassy surface of the wall. It seemed a great deal higher from down here, ScabRat noticed. He wished he were a Fiend, with great, bat-like wings to carry him to the top in a single leap. As well to wish for forgiveness from Above, he realized, and scratched the flaky spot at the base of one horn. "No, I am not going to help you, idiot," he said, recalling the question. "In fact, I shall tear out your heart and eat it while you watch!"

"Will ye now?" said the man, with a queer smile.

He didn't seem alarmed by the threat. Clearly, he was from one of the deeper circles of Hell, where the tortures were nastier. ScabRat experienced a moment of grudging respect. The deep circles were a long way from the upper wall. It took a truly determined soul to get this far. Nonetheless, order must be maintained. Damned souls did not leave Hell. ScabRat smiled to display his jagged black teeth. Then he lunged, swiping viciously with his claws. They slashed the unresisting air.

ScabRat glanced at his empty talons. He looked to his right. Then he looked left, and saw the man standing nonchalantly with his hands by his sides. Peeved, ScabRat bunched his legs and leapt.

His head smacked into the wall, and he saw stars. "Ow!" he yelled, slumping to his knees. "Hold still, you little bastard!"

"If it suits your honour," said the man, the same peculiar little smile playing about his lips.

ScabRat sprang once more. The man remained in place this time, but the results were remarkably similar. Instead of allowing himself to be decently disemboweled, the man swayed slightly, caught one of ScabRat's wrists, and executed a funny little twist. Suddenly, the ground lunged up to smack ScabRat in the teeth, and moments after that he was pinned like a bug, his neck firmly wedged between the prongs of his own fork.

ScabRat knew he wasn't the smartest of demons. However, he felt his native cowardice often made up for his lack of good sense, and in this case, the message was loud and clear. "I give up," he squeaked. "Who the Hell are you?"

The pressure on the fork eased minutely. "Captain Bernard Devlin MacFlannery, late of the Spanish Foreign Legion, at your service. More or less, anyhow," said the other with a chuckle. "Now, supposing I let you up—will you help me over that wall?"

ScabRat sighed. "No," he said, with uncharacteristic honesty. "You've got the better of me for the moment, but you don't frighten me nearly as much as SuckBowel, my supervisor. I hate to think what he would do if he found out I had let a soul escape. And he would find out, you know. They always do."

The fork lifted, and ScabRat sat up, massaging his neck. MacFlannery regarded him oddly. "Escape from Hell?" said the man. "What in the blazes gave you that idea?"

With a theatrical roll of his eyes, ScabRat waved a talon at the wall. "You're telling me it's simple curiosity prompting you?"

"Never," said MacFlannery. "But I'm not escaping. I'm trying to get in."

ScabRat stopped moving altogether. He blinked, very slowly. "Get . . . in to Hell," he said. The notion was entirely new to him.

"Yes," said MacFlannery earnestly. "I'm dead. I'm a sinner, and I'm dead. I should be in Hell."

"You *want* to go to Hell," said ScabRat. He glanced over his shoulder, realizing for the first time that he could see the traditional Abandon All Hope inscription incised at regular intervals in the obsidian of the wall. They *were* on the outside! MacFlannery had been trying to break in, not out! The demon goggled at the man. "Are you mad?"

"No," said MacFlannery. "I'm Catholic. I've committed many and grievous sins in my life, and now I must burn. It's the *rules*, y' see."

*Totally insane.* ScabRat eyed the pitchfork nervously. *Best to humour him until I can get him back inside. How in name of the Nameless did he get out?* "I can't get you over the wall," he said. MacFlannery shifted his weight slightly, and ScabRat held up his talons. "But I can lead you to the gate," he jabbered. "It's a bit of a walk, of course."

"I've come quite some way already," said MacFlannery. "A little more walking won't hurt me. After all, I'm dead, right?"

"Never met anybody down here who wasn't," said ScabRat, with what he hoped was an ingratiating grin. "Other than the Fallen, that is. Like me," he added, in case MacFlannery had missed the distinction. "Demons. Devils. You know. The ones in charge. With the forks and the whips." He stared pointedly at the trident which MacFlannery still held. Truth be known, ScabRat was rather low on the Hellish hierarchy, having only worked his way up from the ranks of the Larvae a few millennia ago. The pitchfork was his symbol of office and authority, and it meant rather a lot to him. Watching MacFlannery handle its heat and weight without obvious discomfort (or even respect!) depressed him.

MacFlannery ignored the longing gaze with which ScabRat favoured his ironmongery. "If we go to this gate, I'll be taken in properly, will I? They'll send somebody to judge me and organize a real punishment?" He seemed quite anxious about the whole punishment thing.

ScabRat nodded vigorously. "I'm sure of it," he lied. Hell being Hellish, the bureaucracy was bound to screw things up. Practically nobody who arrived was punished for their own sins. Most of them weren't even punished under their own names. What difference did it make anyhow? Damned was damned, so far as ScabRat was concerned. He had never really understood the queer half-pride with which so many souls invested the litany of their sins.

MacFlannery appeared to be satisfied. "After you," he said affably, falling in behind ScabRat. He did not, however, return the pitchfork . . .

Very much later, the two arrived at a set of vast, iron gates. ScabRat was no longer in the lead. Inhuman vitality or not, it took a great deal of energy to propel a two-metre tall, monstrously muscled body over a plain of baking stone. It had been quite some time since ScabRat had been forced to do any serious marching, and he was feeling the strain.

"Wait for me," he whined, as MacFlannery surged ahead.

MacFlannery paused. "What for? Do I need you for some reason?"

ScabRat frowned. He raised a talon, and frowned again. "No," he said at last, having considered the situation carefully. "No, I don't suppose you do. Just tell the recording demon at the gate who you are, and they'll sort you out. Only give me back my fork first."

"I don't think so," said MacFlannery thoughtfully. "Not just yet." He studied the tremendous gates.

*That ought to give him something to think about,* thought ScabRat, enjoying the view. *That's real craftsmanship there.*

They were truly Hellish gates. Higher by half again than the wall itself, the gates were guarded by twisted towers of obsidian, and intricately worked with images of torment. Across the top of the gates, the inevitable "Abandon All Hope Ye Who Enter" motto was worked in flaming letters as tall as a man. They were fearsome gates; terrifying gates; gates designed expressly to alert new arrivals to the seriousness of their situation.

MacFlannery scratched his bulbous nose. "Why are they hanging at that funny angle, then?"

ScabRat deflated. "Bit of an accident," he said. "We mostly use the little postern gate nowadays."

MacFlannery grinned. "Accident wouldn't have happened about two thousand years ago, would it?" He laughed at ScabRat's obvious discomfort. "No need to look so surprised. I was a proper altar-boy in me youth. I know all about the Harrowing of Hell."

"Before my time," lied ScabRat, and stamped off towards the postern gate. With luck, he'd be able to slip back inside unnoticed while the Guardians dealt with the madman. *Otherwise I'm in the deep shit. Or possibly the boiling acid. Which one is it for dereliction of duty? I can't recall . . .*

The madman in question swaggered up to the postern gate, pushing to the front of the enormous line of damned souls. The man who had been about to confess his sins to the Recording Demon shrugged his shoulders and stepped aside without demur. Pressed flat against the wall nearby, ScabRat eavesdropped.

"MacFlannery," said the madman loudly. "Bernard Devlin Mac-Flannery. Catholic." ScabRat didn't catch the reply, but it must have been less than satisfactory, because MacFlannery went on, raising his bullish voice. "I don't care what it says in yer book. I'm a feckin' sinner, I'm feckin' dead, and I intend to feckin' burn for it as a good Catholic should. Now, are yis going to let me in?"

There was another pause. Then MacFlannery said: "Of course I'm a feckin' sinner. I should know, shouldn't I? What about that thing with the nun, the rottweiler and the superglue? If that wasn't a sin, they should be rewritin' the rules. And the business with the bomb and the baby carriage." His tirade paused, then resumed. "Oh, well—and did your mister cleverboots leave the baby in the carriage too? No? I thought not. Tell you what, if you can't find any of me sins in your feckin' book, just let me take a look over, like this . . . "

There was an unearthly howl of pain and rage. ScabRat enjoyed a delightful frisson in his spine. *Steal my fork, will he? Sounds like he's enjoying his first taste of real Hellfire.* ScabRat snarled happily at the man whom MacFlannery had pushed out of line, appreciating the way the damned soul cringed before his hell-spawned visage. His self-image suitably reinforced, ScabRat sauntered through the gate, aiming to slip past the Recording Demon while it was busy with MacFlannery's entrails.

Unfortunately, as he rounded the corner he saw MacFlannery ripping the fork from the scaly hand of the Recording Demon. A flood of steaming ichor vomited from the awful wound, hissing as it oozed over the Book. "Oh, crap!" said ScabRat. Then he felt a rising glee. "Hey," he bellowed, over the wails of the Recording Demon, "You stained The Book! They're really going to get you for that one, Mac-Flannery!"

"Right," shot back MacFlannery over his shoulder. "More eternity,

Put it on me feckin' tab." Then he hefted the pitchfork and swaggered into the very mouth of Hell itself, whistling a jaunty little tune.

"Call Lower Down," muttered ScabRat as he slunk past the Recording Demon in MacFlannery's wake. "We've got a situation here."

Situation indeed. MacFlannery was already making himself popular with the Guardians of the Gate by the time ScabRat found his way onto the scene. One of the Guardians—a true Fiend, with wings and horns and scarlet skin—lay supine, clutching his gouged crotch which streamed thick, black ichor. While ScabRat gaped, MacFlannery flung the fork straight and true, downing the second Guardian with a colossal thud.

The final Guardian landed a safe distance away and uncoiled its whip. MacFlannery didn't wait. As the black whip snaked out, the stocky man dropped his head low, shielding his face in his arms. The whip coiled about his belly, but even as the Fiend yanked with Hellish strength, MacFlannery charged. Taken by surprise, the Guardian staggered, and MacFlannery closed in. Binding a coil of the whip, he leapt upwards, planted a foot on the horny knee of the Guardian, and slung a loop like a noose around the thick neck. The momentum of his charge carried him clean past the Guardian, and his weight tightened the noose with a snap. As ScabRat gaped, the Guardian staggered again, and fell clawing futilely at its own throat.

Even before it hit the ground, MacFlannery closed in, balanced wide-legged. As the Guardian fell, MacFlannery heaved on the whipcord. There was a wrenching snap. The Guardian spasmed once, then flopped bonelessly to the courtyard. Except for the fading screams of the partially eviscerated Guardian, there was a stunned silence.

"Is that the best you've got, then?" inquired MacFlannery of ScabRat, who backpedalled rapidly.

"Hey," hissed ScabRat at the Recording Demon, who was attempting to bind his torn talon. "Where are the rest of the Guardians?"

"We've never needed more than three before. The rest were shifted Deeper Down a millennium back. In case you hadn't noticed," snarled the Recording Demon, "It's been getting crowded around here. We're shorthanded."

"Shorthanded," brayed MacFlannery, pointing at the Recording Demon. "That's a good one, that is. You're a funny bastard, aren't ye?" Chuckling, he strolled across the courtyard and wrenched the iron fork from the downed Guardian. "Here," he said to ScabRat. "I thought you lot were immortal. This bag of shite looks about as dead as dead gets."

"Immortal, sure," said ScabRat, eager to stay on the good side of anybody who could demolish three Fiends in as many breaths. "So are you. We're all immortal down here. Doesn't mean we can't get hurt. Or discorporated. Those three will be down amongst the Larvae now, working their way back up through the ranks." He sidled over to the Fiend with the broken neck. Making sure that MacFlannery wasn't watching, he quickly freed the whip. Then he yelped as the needle-like hooks tore at his leathery palm. "It'll take them a century or two," he said, sucking at his stinging hand, "When they get back, they're going to be really angry with you."

MacFlannery regarded ScabRat. "You keep saying such things as though they matter, devil. D'ye not yet understand? I'm damned! I'm here for all eternity. What's an angry devil more or less?" He strode across the distance between them and shot out a powerful hand, grabbing one of ScabRat's horns and forcing the Bounderer's head down to eye level. "With that much time, I'll be making every last one of you angry eventually. It's just the way I am."

ScabRat wrenched himself free. Only his native cowardice and the sight of three freshly discorporate Fiends kept him from lunging for MacFlannery's throat. Never before had he been so enraged by a dead soul. MacFlannery had a rare talent. Still, there were things about Hell which MacFlannery simply couldn't know, ScabRat realized. "There's worse down here than those," he asserted. "Look behind you, if you doubt it!"

MacFlannery sidestepped sharply, planting his back against the wall. Hovering above the courtyard, there was a kind of dark brightness, an indescribable shimmer—and a definite, powerful sense of presence.

I am come, said the dark shimmer voicelessly. Anaphael of the Judges.

Something flip-flopped in ScabRat's belly. *I've never even seen one of the Judges before,* he realized. *This is getting way out of hand.* Quickly, he shuffled backwards through the dust, feeling behind him for the exit.

"Y' look like a cheap special effect," said MacFlannery, his lip curling. "Steven Spielberg wouldn't piss on ye."

ScabRat whimpered, covering his eyes. If he was lucky, the blast of Hellfire would only sear his eyelids, and he wouldn't have to wait through months of blindness to regrow his eyes.

Bernard Devlin MacFlannery, said the thing. Your name is known to me.

"I should feckin' well hope so," growled MacFlannery. "Yer lad at the door thought otherwise, mind. And yer fool doorkeepers obviously didn't know shite, or they might still be breathing. Or whatever."

ScabRat essayed a peek, unable to believe his ears. Why wasn't MacFlannery a smoking cinder?

You have not yet been judged, MacFlannery, said Anaphael with his voice of tearing silk. Nor yet can you be judged, for your name has not been entered in the Book of Sins. I know not why this is so, but I shall rectify the matter. Therefore I place this weird upon you, Bernard MacFlannery: that you shall pass through the circles of Hell until you come to the Place of Judgement. That when you arrive, your name shall be entered in the Book of Sins, and you shall be properly adjudged. That you will thenceforth suffer rightly for your sins for all eternity, as it is written.

"Where's this place of judgement, then?" MacFlannery thrust his chin forward. "How do I get there? Is there a bus?"

Follow that one, spoke Anaphael. A searing whiteness arced down, striking fire against ScabRat's chest. ScabRat gave a cry and beat frantically at the dancing flames which burned without consuming. {And Bounderer,} the voice continued, ringing inside ScabRat's head, {Bring him slowly. Let him see all that awaits him. Let him know the full measure of fear and despair that is Hell, that he may beg for mercy—and let him learn then the mercy of damnation!}

"Beg for mercy. Right," muttered ScabRat as the malevolently beautiful shimmer vanished. "No problem."

"What are you talking about?" said MacFlannery.

ScabRat eyed the man for a long moment, thinking of the sights ahead. Boiling blood. Rivers of excrement. Horror piled upon unspeakable horror; all the torments of the damned. "Nothing much," he said, with a happy smile. "Ready for a little walk?"

"Lead on, MacDuff," misquoted MacFlannery. "Damned be he who first cries—oh, wait. Bit late for that, eh?"

                                    *

A timeless time later, ScabRat the Bounderer burst into the Place of
Judgement, running as though pursued by Avenging Angels. "Beg for
mercy," he panted, as he slammed the vast doors behind him and
wrestled the huge iron bar into place. "Know the fear and despair of
Hell!" Swiftly, he seized a pike from a bemused Fourth Circle Shib-
boleth and wedged it into the crack at the bottom of the door. Turning
to the assembled Demon Judges, ScabRat bellowed: "Where in Hell
is Anaphael?"

In the back of his mind, he knew that shouting at Lords of Hell
was something the old ScabRat would never have done, but since
meeting MacFlannery, the old ScabRat had somehow given way to a
harder, more desperate character. The fiendish visages of the Judges—
as potent an assembly of pure evil as ever he had seen—which once
would have turned his bowels to water now simply irritated him.
"Are you all deaf? I asked for that idiot Anaphael!"

I am here, said the shimmering creature, drifting between a huge
blob of putty covered with silently screaming mouths and a gigantic,
fanged squirrel in a yellow trench-coat. You will spend aeons burning
as a Larva for this, little one.

"Tell it to the marines," said ScabRat. His vocabulary had
expanded too. "Listen, I've brought your boy MacFlannery. And it
was no easy job."

MacFlannery, said Anaphael. I know this name. He was not
judged. You have brought him?

"More or less," shrugged ScabRat. "I don't think he'll be begging
for mercy, though."

You showed him the torments of Hell?

"Started with the boiling blood," said ScabRat. "Even showed him
his father, halfway out in the lake."

And—?

ScabRat shook his head. "He waded knee-deep into boiling blood
so he could brain his own father with a rock. Then he nailed the old
man to the bottom of the lake with a fork and left him there. Said he
*owed* him." The Bounderer folded his arms. "Want to hear what happened when we found his mother? She was being flayed by an Ifrit
with a red-hot razor. MacFlannery said it wasn't good enough. He said

he'd seen something once in Northern Africa, and then he whispered something to the Ifrit, and the poor thing screamed and ran off. He's been places, this MacFlannery. Wars. Riots. Incursions. He's told me about things. Napalm. Cluster munitions. Nerve toxins. And us, with our whips and our chains—you know what he says about us? He says there's men who pay money to be treated that way! Says it's how they have sex!" His voice rising to a shriek, ScabRat stamped his taloned foot. "He called us a bunch of silly perverts!"

A ripple of consternation went around the tremendous hall.

We feared this, said Anaphael. Humans were granted the Divine spark of creation denied us. For millennia we have striven to learn—but they are so very many, and in the end, we are only what we are.

"Now you tell me," said ScabRat. "Well, I hope you've got some kind of contingency plan. MacFlannery found a bunch of men from his old unit down amongst the murderers and the traitors. And they were already planning a breakout, you see. Apparently, if you combine sulphur from all the brimstone around here with potash from the rivers of shit, and mix it with powdered charcoal you get something called—"

With a roar, the doors of the Place of Judgement shattered into a thousand shards and blasted the room with lethal shrapnel. From the cloud of smoke poured dozens of figures brandishing an array of vicious weapons. Some hurled skulls which burst with almost Hellish flame where they struck. Others leveled metal tubes which belched fire and spat lead. Still others waved pitchforks, whips, swords, pikes and all the paraphernalia of Hell. At the forefront strode MacFlannery himself in the ebon armour of a Fifth Circle Nemesis. His face was black with soot, but his teeth gleamed in a madman's grin. His hair and beard stood out like a fallen halo, and the twists of gunpowder woven into it smoked and hissed as he advanced.

"Have at 'em lads," he howled. "Let's show these Nancy-boys some real Hell!"

From behind the wreckage of a bench, the screaming putty-blob reared up and struck at MacFlannery. Still grinning, he whipped an enormous blunderbuss from behind his back and shoved it into a handy orifice. There was a muffled thump. Sticky greenish goo showered the hall, and MacFlannery swaggered on.

Sheltered in a corner, ScabRat blinked at the sudden discorporation of one of Hell's lesser Lords. *That's gotta hurt,* he thought, pulling up the remnants of a throne to watch in comfort.

A towering scorpion with the head of a lion and two rows of perfect breasts died in a hailstorm of lead, stinging the one damned soul it had managed to seize. A floating head the size of an elephant vomited a black wave of tiny, lethal spiders that swarmed over the Damned. Then the spiders were swallowed up by a rolling wall of ersatz napalm that smelled of pitch and human fat. The giant head floated upwards, but a primitive cannon of brass and chitin roared, and the head disintegrated into a hundred disgusting fragments, raining down on the combatants.

It was utter chaos in the Place of Judgement, but it was not pandemonium, ScabRat realized. In fact, the Damned seemed to be making pretty good headway. Still, it couldn't last. The Judges were only of the middle and lower orders of Hell's rulers. For the time being, the melee was fun to watch, but sooner or later, somebody important was sure to take notice. Somebody like—

*HOLD!*

And they did, Damned and Judges alike. Even MacFlannery left off gouging out the dozen-odd eyeballs of the chittering thing he was fighting, and turned very slowly to face the Being in the shattered doorway.

Shining with a terrible light, the great, winged form inclined its head to enter the Place of Judgement. From behind a shattered plinth, one of the Damned dared stretch an arm to hurl a fireskull—and simply vanished in an eyeblink, blasted to ash by the gaze of the First Fallen.

*BERNARD DEVLIN MACFLANNERY.*

MacFlannery staggered, and sank to one knee.

*At last,* thought ScabRat. *About bloody time!*

*WE KNOW THEE, MACFLANNERY.*

"I should bloody well hope so," said MacFlannery, narrowing his eyes. He rose to his feet with a visible effort. "I've been trying to get some service around this place for an eternity."

*THOU ART WRONGLY IN THIS PLACE, MACFLANNERY. DEPART.*

"Now wait a minute," said MacFlannery. "I've come a long way to be judged and punished for my sins, and I'm not going to be sent on me way like . . . like . . . what do you mean, 'wrongly in this place'? I'm as black a sinner as ever the world has seen!"

TRUE. YET STILL THOU MUST DEPART, FOR THOU ART NOT YET DEAD.

"Not . . . dead? Of course I'm feckin' dead. If I'm not dead, what am I doing down here?"

DRINK HATH CAST THEE INTO A SLUMBER LIKE UNTO DEATH. THY SOUL HATH WANDERED UNTIL NOW. ONCE MORE WE BID THEE DEPART, MACFLANNERY.

"Dead drunk? Of course! Yes, I remember now." He looked down at his body, which was growing more insubstantial by the second. "So this is some kind of warning, like in the stories? I'm supposed to change me ways or I'll wind up with the Damned in Hell?"

IT MAY BE SO.

"Bollocks," spat MacFlannery. He shook a fading fist at the terrible, radiant figure that loomed over him. "I'll be back, you bastard. D'ye hear? Bernard MacFlannery will be back, and then God help yis all!"

The armour of the Nemesis, suddenly empty, clattered to the floor. For some time, the First Fallen stared inscrutably at the place where MacFlannery had been. At last, raising his shining head, he spoke a Word and banished the sundry Damned from the shattered hall. Then he sat on a pile of rubble and fell into a kind of brown study, while the remaining Judges began the task of putting matters to rights.

Greatly daring, ScabRat approached. "Excuse me, Lord," he said. "Can I ask something?"

THOU ART—?

"ScabRat, Lord," he lowered his gaze. "A Bounderer, usually."

SPEAK, BOUNDERER.

Hesitantly, ScabRat glanced upwards, shielding his eyes from the awful light. "What he said at the end . . . about coming back. Was it true?"

There was a long pause, and ScabRat cringed, at last fully realizing who it was that he was addressing. Just as the Bounderer was about to slink off into the darkness, there came a reply.

YES.

ScabRat quivered. "And what Anaphael said. About humans having the creative spark, and us trying to learn from them . . . that was true too?"

IT IS SO.

A bleak picture formed in ScabRat's mind; an image of MacFlannery, of a thousand MacFlanneries; a million MacFlanneries pouring into Hell in an endless stream. "What . . . what shall we do, Lord?"

ALL THAT WE CAN DO, BOUNDERER.

"What is that, Lord?"

PRAY. WE CAN PRAY FOR THEIR SOULS.

Then the First of the Fallen vanished, leaving ScabRat alone and afraid.

# EYE CONTACT

## BY MONICA J. O'ROURKE

She tested the strength of the restraints and found them alarmingly secure. She yanked and kicked but barely moved, yet somehow expected a bout of strength. It never came.

He was peering in at her through the bubbled glass of the doors to the long-abandoned basement lab. Leaning against the door, that shit-eating smirk plastered across his face. Tormenting her with those snake-like, heavy-lidded eyes.

Screaming was useless through the gag. Crying was useless because her nostrils quickly filled up.

Had she made eye contact? She tried to *beg* with her eyes, tried to reach into his hollow hull of a body, caress his rustling husk of a soul. She withdrew her hand and came out grasping dead leaves and rotting mulch.

Bones littered the floor. To her left, a tibia. A metatarsal on the right. Skeletal hands hung in chains, suspended by yellowed, cracked joints; a broken radius, a dislocated carpometacarpal joint. Pre-med offered her knowledge of anatomy, but no comfort. She looked at the bones with a pervasive dread.

He was her Bio professor. He'd instructed her, had been a nurturing and guiding teacher. She'd trusted him. No reason not to.

Beside the rust-stained sink and filth-covered toilet, the bathtub was filled with a murky, viscous liquid that smelled like the Bio lab itself—feral, musky, like disease, like decaying rodents. Wafting odours like the butcher department in a supermarket. A dry, meaty smell. She'd craned her neck to see what was submerged in the tub. What appeared to be a human foot was jutting through the surface, and she didn't want to know what else was under that black liquid.

Her body had gone numb, her mind following. Fear was something of a distant memory. Reality refused to settle in her brain, although it gnawed away like a rat burrowing in the soft palate. She could only wish for death. She suspected that fear would return soon enough. For now, she would savour the numbness.

She rattled the chains again, trying to get his attention. The way he sat there, clipboard in hand, pen poised to jot notes, was infuriating.

His staring was making her insane. It felt like she had ceased to exist, that maybe he was looking at her remains. What was he seeing?

She stared back, challenging him. *Come on and get it over with,* she willed at him. *Coward! Untie me and—*

Chains rattling, limbs aching, vision blurry with freshly spent tears, she slumped back.

Hope. There must always be hope. He hadn't killed her. Maybe he would let her live.

Maybe—

She held his stare and finally looked away, her eyes unable to resist blinking. She looked back. He was still staring. Still sitting in his chair.

Just staring at her.

Slumped against the glass, his lips practically kissing it. But no hot breath steamed the glass.

She screamed into her gag, choking on the tears and mucus that filled her nostrils.

His dead eyes met hers and never looked away.

# THE GREAT MELODY

## BY SIMON KEWIN

It is the evening of the 10th of December, 1795, in the small, snow-bound, Bavarian town of Jenzburg, where a local musician by the name of Franz Kraft has just knelt down at his own fireside to pray. Apart from the wavering, red glow sent out by the fire, he is in complete darkness. His eyes are closed. He savours the warmth from the fire on his face for a moment before he starts, whilst behind him, unseen, monstrous, shifting shadows are projected onto the walls of his room. Outside, only the bright, frosty stars light the world. The bell of a nearby church rings out, its tone brittle and cold in the thin night air, calling the people of Jenzburg to worship.

He is a moderately successful man by the standards of his time and place. He makes a living by giving music lessons to the children of the local aristocracy. Sometimes, when their regular conductor is indisposed, he leads a local ensemble in performances of popular orchestral works and is able to earn himself a little extra money. And occasionally he receives commissions to arrange well-known pieces to suit the needs of particular musicians, providing himself with a further, if rather unreliable, source of income. This latter is something he particularly loves to do, although there is always a faint discord of resentment sounding at the back of his mind when he does so. But the earnings from all of these activities give him an acceptably comfortable life and allow him to rent spacious, furnished apartments in a part of town only slightly past its best.

He has every reason, then, to be satisfied with his life. And yet

Franz Kraft is a discontented man. The reason for this is his growing feeling that old-age is encroaching, day by day dulling the verve and zest that once seemed to fill him. He is fifty-two years old, a decent age given the life-expectancies of his time. And he simply feels from time to time, tonight being one such time, that his own death is looming near. He catches the occasional glimpse of its terrible inevitability in shadows cast across an old wooden doorway, or in the weathered, lichened stonework of one of Jenzburg's churches. He is tormented by thoughts that it will not be long before his gravestone is cut, and carved with its two dates, and placed with finality at the head of a freshly-dug grave, ultimate and unavoidable like the final bar-line at the end of a musical score. And then all that will be left of him in the world is his name on the stone, becoming slowly more unreadable with each passing year, until ultimately it fades into illegibility.

He has never married and so has no children to carry on his name or to hear his ideas and thoughts about the world. He is a religious man, indeed Christian doctrine is utterly central to his being, and he knows, with an absolute certainty, that he will attain an eternal afterlife in heaven when he does die. But this provides him with a curiously small amount of comfort. It is perhaps guilt about this, and a desire for confession, that is a part of the reason he is kneeling down and praying tonight.

But also, there is something more. For tonight he is going to pray to God for help in achieving the continuance of his life on Earth. A means by which his name can live on after his death. A sort of indirect and vicarious form of immortality. Not that he is going to ask God for anything at all unreasonable—not an extension to his allotted number of years on Earth, or anything presumptuous of that sort. His position is simply this.

For years, for all of his adult life, he has composed music—beautiful music, stirring music, exultant music. Music glorying God, praising God, worshipping God. This has been his life's work, his love, his passion. And truly he has not done any of it for his own benefit or to elevate himself. His devoutness and pious sincerity is total. But with his departure from the world imminent, the thought that all of his music might go unheard, might be forgotten, is weighing upon him more and more. For he has never succeeded in achieving the recognition as a composer he knows he deserves and there is a very real danger, he knows, that he never will.

This is the crux of the whole matter. This is the truly unbearable thought for him. It is really this that drives him to prayer tonight. Desperately, passionately, he wants his music to live on after he has gone.

Sometimes he feels that it is vanity to wish for such recognition. But, he reasons with himself, there is something in all of us which hopes we will be remembered after our deaths. Others build great buildings, or sit alone writing stories in the hope that others will one day read them. Perhaps it is just the natural urge to reproduce and carry on the species, sublimated and transformed. Perhaps it is the unbearableness of thinking that we will depart the world utterly and forever when we die. But whichever, Franz Kraft knows that his desire is really no sin. It is something very deep in him, but it feels whole-some, not some temptation of the devil. It feels to him like a part of the way in which God has made him.

And so, feeling guilty at asking what he is asking, but going ahead anyway, he begins. It is, in fact, the first time he has ever requested anything from God for himself.

"Oh God, the almighty, the beneficent, grant me, I beseech thee . . . "

He kneels there for a long while, silently mouthing his prayers, pouring out his soul. Outside, on the narrow, icy, sleigh-furrowed streets of Jenzburg, there is a brief flurry of human activity as the evening service in the nearby church comes to an end, and then the calm and quiet returns. For an hour or more he kneels, lost in his earnest supplications.

And then, suddenly, it seems to him that God answers. There are no definite words as such, but he finds himself overwhelmed by a feeling of absolute, reassuring calm and at the same time, a rich, sweet, wondrous thrill such as he has not felt since he was a child, discovering snow or music or love for the first time. And then the music begins in his head. Franz Kraft hears the voice of God singing to him.

In his mind, the heavenly melody slowly unfurls: flowering and glorious like the most colourful of all sunrises; as beautiful as the trees of the forest after snow as the moonlight illuminates them; as deeply pleasing as the babbling of secret mountain brooks. Sixteen perfect notes, in perfect, glowing succession. The divine voice rich, delicate and exquisite. Bass, tenor, alto and treble all at once.

At the breathtaking beauty of the notes, tears come to Franz Kraft's eyes. Such a simple melody, but more glorious, more uplifting than he ever would have thought music could be. Now that he hears it, he knows that it will be in his mind forever; that it will weave itself in and around his thoughts and feelings for all of his days to come; that all other music will now seem pale and superficial by comparison. Moved, awed, glorying, stunned into silence by sheer ecstasy, he kneels in silence.

He remains there for a long time, lost in wonder at the divine gift, whilst the fire before him burns slowly down to its embers, fading from red to yellow to grey. The Great Melody, the sixteen great notes, glide and thrill through his mind still, more and more glorious each time he hears them.

And slowly, his thoughts turn to the technical matters of writing the music down. In his mind, intermingled with his feelings of religious awe, he hears more sounds. Variations on the sixteen notes. Progressions which diverge into different melodies. A great crescendo where finally, at the end, the great notes are played in their entirety, almost unbearably grand and moving.

Soon, in an hour or so, as a grey ghost-light starts to drift out of the Bavarian snow, he will look up from his prayers and, dreamlike, pick up his quill and paper to commence the great work. Throughout the whole of tomorrow he will sit at his desk, scrawling musical notes onto blank bar-lines. Fervently, almost frenzied, he will work, writing as quickly as his fingers will allow, desperately trying to get down the harmonies and melodies that fill his mind before he forgets them. He will write as rapidly as fingers will allow him to, but even so it will not be quick enough to record all of the music he hears. Long into the next night, and the day after that, he will sit, allowing himself only the briefest of interruptions, ignoring cold and hunger, working and reworking each passage of the music and wishing he had ten hands to write with.

Over the weeks, months and years to come, it will be like this often for Franz Kraft. The intense creative impulse that burns in him now, the impulse that usually lasts only for a day or two will come to consume him completely. He will become so engrossed in his task that it will utterly dominate his life. His music lessons and other activities will slowly fall by the wayside and he will end up working only enough to allow himself to subsist. He will withdraw from the world, mindless of what events occur around him, until he becomes all but a hermit. His rooms, and indeed he himself, will become unkempt and dishevelled. But none of this will matter to him—he will want only to be at his desk, working on his masterpiece.

In fact, he will now live on for quite a long time. His fears about his imminent death are unfounded. He will have twelve more years of life in Jenzburg, and will spend almost every waking moment of them working at his task—writing music, rewriting music, arranging music, tearing up music that is not quite right. He will never, in fact, achieve the recognition he hopes for on Earth. He will never live to see any of his works published. But he will stop dwelling on the possibility and will now live out his remaining years engrossed in his work, and happy enough. He will become slowly poorer, but he won't mind. Indeed, he will barely notice.

And when he finally does die, at the fine old age of sixty-four, the great work, the High Mass, will be there, completed. At the very end, it will be only the creative effort of it that sustains him. He will die soon after the task is completed, like a man who loses a beloved wife of many years and loses also the will to live.

It is on another cold winter's night, like that of twelve years previous, that he steps uncertainly out onto the icy, deserted streets of Jenzburg—an old man now, a little crooked and a little uneven in his walk. The snow he slips and toils through is feet deep; it has taken him all of his strength to force his front door open against the barricading snow-drift and he is breathing very quickly now in short, shallow, panicky breaths. He makes his way slowly up the street, leaning into a wind that seems to sliver the skin from his bones.

Clutched to his chest he carries the manuscript of the High Mass—several hundred sheets of musical score bound into a simple parchment folder. Only one thought now fills his entire universe—to bring the work to the nearby church and place it upon the altar where others will be able to find it. Then his music, the music of God, will be passed on. It will live. His great labour will be complete. There is no doubt in his mind that it only needs people to see and hear the work for this to happen. He knows it to be the greatest, most profound, most beautiful musical ever composed.

The cold is intense. It cuts through his thin clothing and seems to turn his bones into icicles. Single-mindedly, seeing only the church down the street ahead of him, he trudges on. A warm, yellowy light flickers out from the church's windows—light from the candles lit within. But his progress is slow; it begins to seem that he is achieving no forward motion at all, as if the snow is absorbing each step like sand, or as if the bitter wind is deliberately holding him back. The church up ahead never seems to get any nearer. For a dizzying, disorientating moment, it actually seems to be moving further away from him, receding backwards down the street.

There is only one thing he can do. He strides on. There is nothing left for him in the world but to get to the sanctuary of the church. God has given him this great music; God will see that he is allowed to complete the task. After a few more paces, he finds that he is no longer feeling the cold—indeed that a warmth is starting to spread throughout his body. He finds that he can no longer feel the terrible, biting cold in his feet, as if he is no longer walking on the ground. Water fills his eyes and the light from the church smears and becomes nothing but an indistinct blur. He closes his eyes to try and clear his vision.

There is another moment of disorientation, and a taste of cold water is suddenly in his mouth. He opens his eyes to find that he is lying on the ground, half buried in the snow where he has fallen. With one of his eyes he can see nothing but a grey whiteness; with the other he can see along the street. A few yards away, out of reach now, the manuscript lies on the snow. Beyond it, in a direct line from where he lies, the lights from the church waver above the ground. Slowly the scene fades as his eyes close, but there is no despair in him. He knows that his body will be found, that the work will be found, the both of them waiting there upon the pristine snow. His music will live.

And then Franz Kraft sees no more.

After a moment's pause the wind picks up once again. It opens the folder containing the manuscript of the High Mass. And one after the other, like leaves flying free from a tree, the pages are lifted by the wind and borne away. Some fly over the rooftops of the town. Some drift and flit back up the street. Some rise upwards, off into the icy heavens. Others fall to the ground again and lie scattered around the body of Franz Kraft like strewn flowers.

Tomorrow morning, they will find him there, old Kraft the recluse, locked away in his rooms all these years composing his great, divinely-inspired work, frozen and half-buried in the overnight snow but looking strangely content in his death.

They will lift up his body, and carry it solemnly up the street to the church whilst preparations are made for his interment. Others, meanwhile, will try to gather together the pages of the musical score they find scattered all over the town. In the days to come, many pieces of the work will be collected together—pages found frozen into the ice of the town's lake, or caught in the branches of the trees.

They will try to put all of the pages back together in their proper order, to recreate the High Mass, but it will prove to be impossible. Many of the sheets will remain lost, whole sections and movements missing. Some attempts will eventually be made by local musicians to play those fragments of the work that are recovered, but they will be able to reproduce only tantalising glimpses of soaring, glorious music before coming to a missing section of the work and having to stop. Incomplete, scattered, the Great Melody will be lost to the world.

But it will become a local legend in the town of Jenzburg that, one day, the complete manuscript of Franz Kraft's High Mass will be reassembled. Every now and then, it will be said, another sheet of the music turns up, found in some hidden corner of the town, at the bottom of a chest or between the leaves of other old papers. Like the gradual unfolding of a divine plan, the slow revelation of some great secret, the work will be brought back together piece by piece. And then finally, one day perhaps far into the future, the High Mass, the Great Melody, will be complete once again, to be played and heard.

# THE RANDOM BREAKFAST GENERATOR

## BY PAUL HASSING

Tristan the Advertising Cadet tossed fretfully on his futon. He really needed All Bran this morning. Fifteen days of Froot Loops had left him twitchy, constipated and more than a little paranoid. Once again he fantasised about sabotaging his Smeg Random Breakfast Generator.

'Wallpaper' magazine had claimed that random cereal generation was the ultimate way for young executives to prove their ability to handle whatever life threw at them. The concept was so exclusive that global distribution was restricted to one client per postcode.

Tristan bid furiously online for the personality assessment, triggering a call from his Help Desk Officer, who he told to fuck off. He won the auction, noting in the disclaimer that random generation was not recommended for Capricorns. He earned a borderline pass and secured his order with a massive down payment. At last he had the means to erase office memories of his mother's mortifying muesli porridge deliveries.

After four months' wait and a three day installation nightmare, the Random Breakfast Generator (or RBG as Tristan was now entitled to call it) dominated his apartment. The cost was crippling.

He threw a party and was amazed at the number of work colleagues who came. Guzzling his designer beers, they filed murmuring around the gleaming cylinders of what looked like a monstrous paint-tinting machine. Tristan poured schnapps for the creatives and learned with delight that they'd visited the web address he'd emailed them.

"Twelve months eh, Cobber?" The Art Director swapped looks with his team. 'Reckon you can handle it?'

Tristan refilled the shot glasses. "Piece of piss, Andre; just you wait."

"We'll be monitoring your progress."

"Go for your lives; the website's updated every day . . . "

"We know."

Tristan's favourite Account Coordinator approached the bar, achingly lissom in a Christopher Kronos spray-on. Tottering on her Nine Wests, she hefted Tristan's Orrefors pitcher and sent a sparkling fragment into the salad centrifuge.

"Oops! Sorry Trist; my bad. The Boys said we need another jug of Midori."

Tristan gritted his teeth and emptied another textured bottle. It was Danni, more than anyone, that he wanted to impress.

She put her elbows on the bar and leaned forward smiling. "Nice toy." She flicked her eyes to the RBG. "Cost a bit?"

Tristan's knife missed its lime completely. "Fuck yeah! I mean— yeah. A bit."

"So how'd you manage to pick thirty cereals? I can only think of . . . four."

"They gave me a list of hundreds; I just had to rank them. They had every cereal from round the world. Even ones they don't make any more."

"Yeah?" She took a slice of lemon and stroked it absently over her tongue. "Even Chocco Nuggets?"

Tristan blinked. "Chocco Nuggets? I can't believe you said that! How d'you know about them?"

"I used to have 'em at Grandma's."

"Fair dinkum?"

"Fair dinkum."

"Shit! So did I!"

Danni put the lemon in her mouth and bit hard. Her freckled nose wrinkled. "Wow!"

Tristan stirred the pitcher and tossed in a sprig of parsley. "I put Chocco Nuggets third; I haven't had them for ages; I wouldn't mind if I got them every day."

Danni grinned. "That'd kinda defeat the purpose though, wouldn't it? Still, I'd love to have 'em again one day too."

"You would?"

"Yeah!"

Tristan's heart began to thump. "Well, maybe . . . "

"Oi, Danster!" A large Sales Rep gestured from the balcony. "Tell Ted to hurry up with that fucking jug!" The Sales Boys always called Tristan Ted. Short for Shithead.

"Coming!" Danni grabbed the pitcher. "Gotta go, Trist; great party. I hope you get Chocco Nuggets every day."

Tristan gazed after her, then realised the creatives were staring at him.

The copywriter lifted an eyebrow. "Chocco Nuggets?"

*

Smeg contracts were Draconian by design. Tristan was glad; it was going to take a lot to make up for his failure to stop the Sales Boys pissing in his spa. He scanned the pages over his first random breakfast of Froot Loops, left buttock still aching from his NanoBot injection. In a few hours, the implant would advise Smeg Client Service that Tristan's meal had entered his duodenum and was past the point of return.

Failure to receive this message every 24 hours would elicit a warning. Unless Tristan could prove an eligible medical condition, his contract would be terminated, his huge surety forfeited and his loser status proclaimed on Smeg's RBG microsite. When he arrived at work, he was stunned to see every browser displaying this exact site.

"We're all eager to see how you get on." The Copywriter's breath was hot at Tristan's ear. "We've even organised a little communal bet, if you're feeling confident."

Tristan flushed. "Oh really?" His voice shrilled as heads popped from every cubicle. "You're bloody on!"

A cheer went up and the Copywriter handed Tristan a pen. "Nice one, Squadron Leader, sign here!"

The contract was printed on the studio's best paper. Through smarting tears Tristan beheld a terrifying figure in double bolded comic sans.

Tristan barely slept that night. He was hocked to the eyeballs; if he lost the bet, he'd have to default on his BMW. He glared at the pristine hoppers glinting in the moonlight. Suddenly they gave an unearthly groan and began to rotate. Tristan leapt like a deer, straight through his Japanese changing screen. Then he remembered: the RBG self-cleaned daily. He'd nominated 3:00pm; the cycle was twelve hours early. For fifteen minutes he watched the machine behave like a mantis after feeding. The awful scrapes and whines raised his hackles repeatedly. Thoroughly spooked, he watched his "Lost in Space" videos until it was time for breakfast.

He got Froot Loops.

The probability of two consecutive identical cereals was 1 in 900. This figure appeared in the RBG's metrics monitor, which also advised Tristan that the odds of his next breakfast being Froot Loops were 1 in 2,700. Though tempted to test them, Tristan's contract constrained him to wait until the following day, whereupon his china bowl rang again with little coloured rings.

The same thing happened the next day.

And the next.

He didn't even like Froot Loops. He'd put them thirtieth—too timid to chance the nasty looking offerings from Yemen, Belarus and Chad. The cereal was painfully crunchy. The coating, which could only be dissolved by pancreatic amylase (thereby freeing radioisotopes for NanoBot detection), could be optioned to keep every morsel milk-free. Tristan rued his choice; preference changes were only free at the annual major service. He couldn't believe that having crunchier cereal than anyone else in his suburb had ever seemed like an edge.

After two weeks of the sickly fruit treats, Tristan's bowels became capricious. He called Smeg and a voice synthesiser offered a service visit, provided he undertook to pay for it should no fault be detected. Miserably he pressed '1'. The voice then asked him to confirm his apartment access code so the Technician could plan his or her day without constraint.

That evening, a crisp printout on Tristan's dining table informed him that comprehensive diagnostics had shown the RBG to be in perfect working order. He converted his remaining share options and went to bed defeated. At 3:00am, the self-clean cycle scared the bejesus out of him yet again. Four hours later, the RBG presented him with another pristine serve of Froot Loops. Tristan regarded the bowl white lipped, then flew to the bathroom and smashed it into his chrome toilet. Flush after flush failed to sink the impermeable rings, which bobbed gaily like so many life preservers. Then Tristan's mobile bleeped with a text message:

"Your Smeg RBG bathroom sensor has detected undigested breakfast material. Please remit proof of your medical condition to avoid breach of contract. Get well soon!"

Irradiation did more than keep the RBG's cereals fresh and sterile, it made them easy to track. Tristan sank to his knees and stared long at the strobing sensor peeping from his s-bend. Suddenly it all seemed too much. What was poverty, compared to this hell? In a year or two he'd be back in the black. He'd had enough.

Riding in the office elevator he felt a faint stirring in his guts. His body seemed to be affirming that his decision, however painful, was the right one. The door dinged open and he exited with a faint smile—straight into a phalanx of manic colleagues.

'He's here; he's not sick! Wooo hooo! We're in the money! We're in the money!'

Tristan's image stared from every terminal, a crimson 'WARNING ISSUED' plastered across his Smeg file. The Copywriter began an exponential conga line and Tristan choked as Danni sashayed past—a hairy pair of sales hands at her supple hips.

For dinner, Tristan fished one Froot Loop at a time from his toilet, rinsed it in a bowl of vodka and washed it down with more.

Mountain dawns and ocean sunsets swept unheeded past Tristan's picture windows. The odds of Froot Loops were now so titanic, the metrics monitor expressed them as a formula. In return for a month's free consumables, Tristan had allowed Smeg to run an article on his freakish statistical experience. Now he spent his evenings bitterly declining invitations from chat rooms. Smeg's home page had even begun scrolling up to the minute data and commentary on his progress.

At work the mood was hostile. It was almost Christmas and Tristan's colleagues were sweating on their windfall. Their premature jubilation had soured to resentment at his stubbornness. Surely it was only a matter of time.

The agency mysteriously snared the All Bran account and Tristan was assigned to oversee the national re-brand. Bound by his contract, he dejectedly donated his pallet of freebies to charity.

On New Year's Eve, Tristan breakfasted as usual. Hunched and rocking in the gloom of his filthy kitchen, he failed to notice the puff of powder that followed the Froot Loops through the dispensing chute. Only when his spoon made a gritty crunching sound did he look into the bowl.

Tristan began to tremble, then tore open his curtains to examine the vessel more closely. Under gentle morning sunlight, a faint residue bore witness to a vanished milk tide.

Ten seconds into the New Year, Tristan activated his RBG again. Amid a blaze of re-aimed downlights, his prayers were answered: Froot Loop dust. With a mad cackle he leapt onto his bench and tapped one of the hoppers with a cleaver. The pentatonic note was loud and pure. He hit another, and the sound was the same. Forcing the machine around on its axis, he banged each cylinder in turn, frantically searching for the one that had to be almost empty. But the Italian steel was too thick to permit differentiation.

Undeterred, he loaded his owner's CD and pored over the specifications, then calculated the volume of Froot Loops he'd eaten during the previous months. He carefully rechecked his figures, concluding that there could be no more than five serves of the hateful food left in the machine. If Smeg thought he were going to authorise a refill, they had another fucking thing coming.

That week saw a transformed Tristan. Though pallid and overweight, he cut a commanding figure among his peers. Even the creatives began to look nervous. With each new dawn, Tristan happily devoured a growing portion of dust until only one possible Froot Loops serve remained.

It was Friday. For the first time in months, Tristan followed his peers to the pub. He drank heavily and even shouted a couple of rounds into his social vacuum. In just a few hours, he'd be free. As he got intoxicated, he began baiting the Copywriter and got a pleasing reaction. For once the shoe was on the other foot. He became increasingly bold, thrilling as the Sales Boys congratulated him on his wit. Goading and taunting, he gradually worked the whole room into laughter at the Copywriter's expense—tapping into deep-seated ignorance and jealousy of the creative function. Then the Copywriter's mobile rang and Tristan elatedly accepted his first free drink since joining the agency. When he turned back, the Copywriter's furious face was only centimetres from his.

"Alright, Arsehole, if you're so fucking confident, why don't you double our bet?"

Tristan did a clumsy mental calculation and ended up with his BMW, two weeks' holiday and enough cocaine to dust Danni's entire body. Swayingly he surveyed the assembly, alcohol burning in his ulcerated stomach. Suddenly, all became hushed.

"Doubleall yerbetsh? Yerrr bloody ONNN!"

The cheer was deafening. Tristan smirked at the Copywriter, who toasted him in surprisingly gracious defeat.

The summer sunset moiled huge on the horizon as Tristan slewed into his apartment. Chuckling and dribbling, he tore off his suit and slithered onto his cool Spanish granite. His pupils slid in and out of focus, then abruptly narrowed to pinpricks. At his nose was a tiny plastic toucan.

He scrambled to his feet and seized the mascot. Attached was a letter from Kellogs, thanking him for all the publicity and promising free Froot Loops for the remaining months of his contract.

Underneath was another Smeg printout, confirming that per the recent change in account conditions (as detailed in the brochure emailed to his work), his hopper had been refilled automatically.

Tearing at his face and hair, Tristan ran howling from the giant burning Froot Loop that filled his Western window.

Back at the office, his Help Desk Officer exited Smeg's Client Control Site and deleted her hacker's ID.

'That'll teach you,' she whispered.

# THE DOCTOR'S PILL

## BY DONNA MAREE HANSON

"Come in, Jane," said Doctor Smiley. "Take a seat over here next to me."

Doctor Smiley looked down at the open file on his desk. The notes read: Jane Simpson, eighteen years, four-year history of an eating disorder in conjunction with severe obsessive compulsive disorder pertaining to food and toilet habits. Hospitalised seven times. A letter on file from her general practitioner begging for some assistance before it was too late.

"Hmm," he looked at Jane and estimated that she was five feet, four inches probably five and half-stone or 35 kilos. He looked back down at the file; there were at least ten photos in the file, one of a laughing girl about 50 kilos, the rest, images of Jane in various stages of emaciation. The nurse's scrawl showed her statistics and he smiled slightly, his guess had been spot on. Obviously he had been at this too long.

"So Jane, tell me what can I do for you, that hasn't been done already?"

Jane looked at the Doctor, her cheeks sunken and her eyes dull, "Help me!" A tear escaped her eyes and she tried blinking them back. "Every time I look in the mirror I see a fat person, but my family keep putting me in hospital. I try and eat and when I do I see fat and starve myself."

"I see and do you really believe I can help you?" He regarded her, waiting to see how willing she was to stop her cycle of starvation and bingeing.

Her dull grey eyes shifted uneasily and then she glanced at him quickly, unwilling to hold his gaze. She fidgeted and played with her hair. She didn't answer until the doctor asked her again.

"Yes. You're my only hope."

"Well . . . it happens that I may have something that will help you. However, I have to explain to you that it is a trial and there is no guarantee that the treatment will work."

"Okay, I don't have any other choices," she nodded and kept on nodding.

"You're sure?" As she kept nodding he got out the paper work. There were five forms to sign, his indemnity, the practice indemnity, acknowledgment of the trial, waiver and non-disclosure agreement. He stacked them in neat pile and handed her a pen and then buzzed the nurse to come and witness the signature. Luckily, she was old enough to sign otherwise he'd have to get her guardians to do it.

*

Jane finished signing the forms and watched the nurse apply her squiggle. The nurse looked her up and down and then left. Jane stood up and walked around the room, carefully avoiding contact with any items. She pulled out a sani-wipe from her bag and wiped her hands. She had touched the pen after all.

"Okay Jane, come and sit down and I will explain it all to you."

She sat down quickly; her heart was beating erratically as she realised that she had no idea what horrible treatment this doctor would prescribe. She'd already been to the 'pooh farm' that fed her juices and piled in the enemas and hot water bottles in her rear to purify her, the sedation, the tube feeding. She'd done it all. What could be worse than that? Eating?

"Now, Jane," he pulled out a large pink pill in a vial. "I want you to fill up that glass of water over there and bring it back here. Don't worry it's been sterilised, just be careful when you undo the wrapper."

She did as he asked and he passed the vial to her. "Now, I want you to put the pill in your mouth and swallow. That's right, good girl."

The pill was large and it made her gag, but it went down. Then she looked at the doctor, as if he was a bug in a microscope. Was that it?

She thought it was strange. She waited for him to explain. She sat for half an hour and he still said nothing.

"Good! That should be enough time for the pill to be absorbed. You won't be up-chucking it now." She started when he spoke. He got up quickly and washed his hands. "Come back and see me every month. If the treatment is working we will know by then. Okay."

He put his hand on her back and propelled her out the door. She stopped, digging in her heels. "Is that it? Just a pill?"

"Yes that's it. Radical treatment, but I am sure you can cope with that. It was painless wasn't it?"

"Yeah, but how's it work?"

"I'm sorry, Jane. I am not a liberty to discuss it. It is a trial after all and I have signed an agreement with the drug company, to keep the nature of the pill secret. I know it works with minimal side effects. If you feel there is a problem just come back anytime."

He shut the door and called his next patient. Jane was nudged out of the way as the next patient tried to get through the door.

Jane paid her $250 non-refundable, non-claimable fee and left. She didn't care as her mother had footed the bill. She mused that the doctor was the weirdest she had ever come across. She decided to try and throw the pill up. It might have calories or fat. It was unusual for her to put something like that in her mouth.

She passed two sets of public toilets; none were suitable. She headed for the mall, and went to her favourite cubicle. She pulled out five sani-wipes and wiped the seat, the toilet roll holder and the door nobs. Then she leant over the toilet bowl and tried to puke. Only clear bile came out as a result of her near silent regurgitation. She climbed up on to the toilet seat standing carefully on the toilet paper she had placed there.

She peed. One, two, three, hold then four. Done. She rummaged through her purse and swallowed five laxatives. If she couldn't dislodge the pill she'd purge it before she had time to put on any weight.

The next morning she looked in the mirror. Standing naked she turned slowly noting the fat rolls and the bulges, the array of cellulite. She decided not to eat today she was too fat.

That night she washed carefully in front of the mirror. She looked at her body first and saw the dark smears on her pale skin. He, her father, had touched her there long ago, but she could still see the marks. She was still unclean.

Using pre-boiled water in a sterile bowl. The shower was full of germs and she never used it. She lathered the antiseptic soap all over her body, pushing it in her rear, her vagina, her nostrils and her mouth. She rinsed them out when the burn became unbearable. She used her douche and she felt the hot water cleanse her.

There was a knock, "Fuck off!" she yelled and she was answered by a curse. She loaded the douche again she felt the antiseptic cleanse her and it made her shudder with purity. Then she did her nostrils; the water poured out of her mouth and burned her throat.

She was clean.

She panted, and she glowed. She turned on the heat lamps and waited for an hour for her skin to dry. She looked at herself closely in the mirror. Her vagina fascinated and repulsed her. Her pubic hairs were growing back she would need to wax them again.

She opened the door and walked naked to her room. Her brother spat a curse, "Christ Jane, do you have to do that? You look like a corpse. Your tits have totally sunken down to nothing. I think I'm gonna puke."

She slammed her door and panted on the other side. She laid the tissue paper over her bed and lay down. The light blared brightly and she kept her eyes open as long as possible it helped keep her pure.

She was hungry the next morning and she ate five slices of toast, four rashes of bacon, three fried eggs, two cups of coffee and one orange juice. Then she ran to the bathroom and stripped off her clothes.

She saw herself perfectly thin in the mirror, her perfect flat breasts, bald vagina and thin legs. Perfect.

She went to school and didn't eat lunch and when she returned she went straight to the bathroom. She looked in the mirror and she was fat and disgusting again. She cried, remembering how perfect she had seemed that morning. She raced to the fridge and stuffed her face with left over chicken, baked potatoes and gravy. Her mother found her on the floor with the fridge open and legs splayed apart.

Jane got up and raced out of the room when she heard her mother's distressed call. She locked herself in the bathroom and waited. She paced, trying to estimate how many laxatives she needed to take to counteract the food she had just stuffed in her mouth.

She stripped off her clothes and performed her cleansing ritual. She double douched every where, including her eyes and ears. As she stood under the heat lamp she turned her gaze to the mirror. She looked perfect. Her thin body was like a gentle reed, supple, willowy everything she wanted it to be.

She went to bed and slept. The next morning she was hungry and she ate her breakfast, in the same numerical order. Then she ran to the bathroom and stripped off, her body was still perfect. She smiled and left for school.

Her routine continued and at the end of the month she returned to the doctor's surgery. He looked up at her when she entered, smiled vaguely then returned to his notes.

"Mmm. That's right you're a trial patient. How's things with you?"

Jane smiled brightly her eyes glowing with health.

Jane saw him note down that her breasts were firm and her hips rounded. The doctor estimated that she was now 50 kilos. He wrote a few notes down in her file and checked his estimate with the nurse's statistics.

"Spot on again," he mumbled to himself and then looked up with a start when Jane spoke.

"I'm very well, Doctor. I don't think I need to come again."

"Well. I know you think everything is fine, but you must come back next month. That is part of the agreement you signed. Remember?"

Jane didn't remember, but she nodded anyway and left. She paid her bill and went home. Her mother had been so nice and even her brother's friends were talking to her, as if they liked her instead of treating her as a freak.

The months went by and soon she became disturbed by her brother's comments and her mother's strange looks. The words obese, fat pig and grotesque floated in the air at home, at school and in the street. She couldn't understand it. When she took off her clothes she saw that her body was perfect. She was cured.

Her mother was upset and showed her the labels on the new clothes, size 18 and size 20. They had argument and Jane accused her of trying to drive her crazy—she wasn't fat. Then Jane had a seizure and they called the ambulance.

Doctor Smiley opened the door and ushered Jane in; he had to step back to let her pass. "Come in, Jane, have a seat by the desk. You are looking well, dear."

"Doctor, they said I was obese!"

"Well I wouldn't say that exactly. You're just not thin any more. You wanted a cure and it looks like you have one."

"Doctor, I had a heart attack. The emergency doctor said I had to diet or the fat around my heart would kill me. Tell me it's not true! I can't believe it. My body is perfectly thin."

Doctor Smiley wrote hurriedly in his notes. "I see. Well that is interesting. Are you eating normally now? No more toilet habits?"

"Well I eat good meals and a few snacks now and then. I don't worry about cleaning the toilet any more and I only do some of my cleansing rituals."

His eyebrow lifted a ray of grey and white, "So you think that you are cured?"

"Yes, Doctor, but I am afraid. I don't look fat, but the Doctor showed me the evidence."

Doctor Smiley stood up and paced his hand idly scratching his chin. "This is unprecedented. I wonder what would happen if I gave you another pill." He went to the cupboard and got another pink pill down. Then he wrote furiously in his notes. He eyed Jane warily. "Mmm I estimate that you are now over 100 kilos. I think you are sufficiently cured to stabilise to a normal routine." As if hedging all his bets he handed her the pill.

She took it eagerly swallowed it without water, her puffy mouth closing juicily over the large pill. She stood up and thanked the doctor and left.

The next morning, Jane screamed. She saw herself in the mirror. She had huge breasts and she couldn't see her vagina as her stomach hung down so low. Her rear was encased in two huge cheeks filled with sweat and muck. Her face when she screamed was like an over-sized purple grape. She could see reality. How things really were. She no longer saw what she wanted to see and she didn't like it.

*

Two weeks later two policemen called to see Doctor Smiley, Officer Digby and Officer Wilberforce. He sat back in his chair and placed his reading glasses over his nose.

"Sorry to disturb you, Doctor. Just a few questions regarding Jane Simpson," said Officer Digby.

The doctor buzzed the nurse and requested Jane's file. "Has something happened to Jane?"

Officer Wilberforce spoke and the doctor turned his gaze to him. "She's dead. Suicide."

"Oh! That's terrible. How did she do it? She had a bad heart you know."

"She choked to death on food. In front of her family."

"Oh that's bad. How can I help you? I don't think I can shed any light on the matter."

"You were treating her weren't you, Doctor?" asked Officer Digby.

"Yes for an eating disorder and other related conditions. However, she was cured."

"May we know the nature of the cure, doctor? You see she left a note?" prompted Officer Digby.

"Did she now. Well I cannot divulge the nature of her treatment as she signed waivers to that effect. The nurse will give you a copy of the waiver on your way out."

"You don't want to know what the note said?" asked Officer Wilberforce, unable to keep the surprise from his face.

"Oh I know what the note said."

Both officers sat straighter in their chairs, "What!" they said in unison.

"The note said, 'It worked.'"

"But how could you know that?" said Officer Digby then he wrote hurriedly in his notebook.

"Just a lucky guess. Now if you will excuse me I have a lot of patients to see. Good Day to you."

Doctor Smiley shut the door after the officers and sat down for a nice cup of tea. He noted in Jane's file the event of her death, and then wrote a note to the drug company recommending a second pill when subject returned to ideal weight.

His nurse buzzed announcing his next patient. Her name was

Jill Howard, she was eighteen, long history of eating disorders. He flicked through the various snap shots and saw the general practitioner's letter begging for help.

"Come in, Jill. Come and sit by me."

# REMOTE

## BY PAUL KANE

The office building looks much the same as any other; an amalgam of glass and metal and concrete existing in the same space.

But it hides dark, dark secrets.

Every weekday for the last ten years he has trod its drab corridors, used its lifts and sat in its offices to do his job. Ten years . . . ever since they found out about him. He is walking to his office right now, following the directions though he knows the way blindfolded. First thing Monday morning and his observers will be waiting for him, ready to give him his brief, to run down the company's mission statement. The man takes in very little of his surroundings, as little as possible in fact. They're meant to be drab after all: no pictures on the walls or fancy patterns here. No distractions.

At last he comes to his own office. The number on its varnished wooden door reads: G786. It is not the room number, it is in fact his name . . . Not the name he was christened with, you understand, but the one they gave to him. The one he is known as at work. The one he has begun to think of as his true moniker. He has no idea what the letter or the numbers mean (it's quite possible that his superiors have no idea either) but it is *his*. It belongs to him.

Grasping the smooth metal knob, he opens the door. Inside is a fair-sized rectangular table, around which his observers are seated. There are three of them (and never the same ones twice): a stocky man with bad teeth and a crown of grey-white hair; a very tall light-ginger man with octagonal glasses who has the annoying habit of blobbing his tongue in and out, like a reptile tasting the air; and a middle-aged woman with a kindly face (as is evidenced by the building itself, though, looks can be very deceptive indeed).

The closest to him, tall ginger, rises first. He doesn't say anything, he just points to a manila file at the head of the table. G786 nods and sits down in front of the file, opening it up to glance inside.

The first thing he sees is a colour photograph of a man dressed in military garb, peak cap and sunglasses. There's a name at the bottom, and a short bio. G786 doesn't take any of this in; there's really no need. He doesn't much care anymore. One guerrilla leader is much the same as another, and he doesn't need to know the ins and outs, the justifications (if indeed there are any). All he needs to know is the country, a vague idea of the whereabouts. He flips through the other papers and finds a map of the area, fairly detailed. Though not as detailed as the satellite pictures that come next, pinpointing buildings, guards, watch-towers . . .

The place where this target is located is like a fortress. It would take an expert in security and special operations to infiltrate its defences, and even then a successful strike could not be guaranteed—plus a highly trained operative would be lost. No, it was much better this way. Much more convenient. Much easier. Much easier . . . for them. As for what it was doing to him, well that didn't really enter into the equation, did it?

Last, but not least, there's a scrap of material pinned to the back of the file. This had been very difficult to acquire, cut from one of the target's old uniforms . . . G786's fingers hover over the square of khaki, but then they withdraw—as if almost touching a flame. Not yet, not yet . . .

They allow G786 a further ten minutes or so to look through the reports again. He doesn't really read them, just shuffles through them for the sake of appearances. It is expected of him, so he obliges. He has no choice.

"So . . . When you're ready . . . ?" says the stocky man.

*Ready? He is never ready . . .*

G786 nods, and thin ginger walks over to the window to close the blinds. The slats slice into the bright morning sunlight for a moment, striping the grey walls white and yellow momentarily. Then all the brightness goes away.

Tall ginger finally takes his seat again as G786 passes his hands over the papers, his fingers now seeking out the scrap of material at the back. He closes his eyes . . . and allows the sensations to develop; stops fighting what is supposed to come so "naturally". It always starts off with a tunnel, a rolling spiral of colours, of reds, golds, blues, greens, twisting round and round. He accesses this without any problems at all, letting the tunnel take him away, lead him in the direction his mind needs to travel. At certain points there are crossroads and intersections, but he instinctively knows which ones to avoid and which to take. The feel of the cloth acts like a scent to a sniffer-dog, linking him to his target, allowing him to cut across great distances in the blink of an eye.

The arrival is always slightly more disorientating. It's instantaneous and he's thrown back into the world without warning. Or at least a piece of him is. He sees the base now, the one from the photograph. He slips past alarms and guards without being seen, because there isn't really that much of him to be seen, and he carries on following his senses. He begins to rub the fabric between thumb and forefinger now, centring in on the man from the photograph. Passing through walls, through locked doors without a second thought.

And then here he is. In a room not much bigger than his office. G786 recognises the target immediately; he sits talking to another man in a language G786 doesn't understand. It doesn't matter really what they are saying. All that matters is that a sighting has been confirmed. G786 knows what has to come next, even though he dreads it. In his present form it is simplicity itself to enter the target's body. The method has been left entirely up to him, it can be slow and painful (such as an internal bleed) or fast and merciful (like the popping of a brain cell here or there). But whichever course of action is taken, one thing is for certain—he must exit the body before it is over or risk being trapped inside forever.

It must be done, though. And no matter how much he wavers, G786 knows this. He wants to get it over with as quickly as possible and so goes for the swifter option. G786 ingratiates himself into the target's head . . . and yet he still hesitates just before doing the deed. Even after all this time, there's still a part of him that . . . No, he mentally shrugs this off (no room for a conscience—for emotions). Continues with the operation. A tweak here, a tweak there. Then he gets out.

The other man in the room is quite surprised by what happens next. His superior suddenly clutches his forehead, eyes clicking backwards in their sockets, and falls out of his chair onto the floor. There is an effort made to save him, naturally, and physicians are even called in to help. But none of it will do any good. G786 hangs around just long enough to make sure his mission has been completed successfully (as if there was ever any doubt) and then departs—searches out the tunnel once more for the return journey.

Back in the office his eyes snap open. "It's done," he tells them.

*

That day he is assigned two more cases, with long breaks between each one, before being allowed to clock out (a senior politician who was rising in the ranks far too quickly and becoming far too idealistic for their liking, and an intelligence operative who had defected to the other side—whatever the other side is supposed to be these days). Now it is time to leave. G786 walks to his maroon car in the lot and climbs inside. He pulls out into traffic on the main road, then begins the half-hour drive to the place he calls home, although the significance of the word has long since shrivelled away into nothing. Once, long ago, it had actually meant something. But that was before he had been forced into the programme (ironically by threatening to tear his home life apart), before his talents had been detected by a routine screening, and before they had enhanced his basic abilities with a daily cocktail of drugs. At first it had been just spying missions, the usual stuff for national security; finding out plans and schemes before they could be used. Locating "enemy" safe houses and monitoring the movement of certain key individuals. It hadn't been hard work, in fact he'd almost found himself enjoying it. Not many people could do what he did and at least he was putting it to good use, for the good of his "country". He was also being compensated adequately for his trouble. Looked after.

But then they started to talk about pushing him further. To see what else he was capable of. To train him in other methods and techniques—the kind that weren't so palatable or easy to excuse. To send him on jobs that took a little piece of him away every time he returned . . . That left him feeling cold and numb afterwards, a shadow of a man.

His car journey mirrors the ones he's taken invisibly that day, except instead of a tunnel there is a road—still, the junctions and turn-offs are the same. And one of these brings him to his house, a pretty white abode with net curtains in the windows and hanging baskets over the front door. G786 opens the garage door with the remote control on his key ring, and parks the car inside. He can get to the house proper through a side-door, which opens out into the kitchen.

On the hob is a boiling pan, steam rising in spirals to touch the ceiling. His wife is cooking spaghetti again, as always on a Monday. And he hears singing—sweet singing that should touch his heart—coming from the hallway, and suddenly she is at the kitchen door. Even dressed in jeans and an old sweatshirt, she looks so beautiful. Her long, dark hair cascading onto her shoulders like a waterfall. She blinks with those wide eyes and tries to smile. It is not the smile of yesteryear, the smile that first attracted him to her, that he fell in love with so long ago . . . This is a smile worn away by heartache and pain.

"Hello, Simon." That's G786's real name. It feels as alien to him now as the house he's in, the woman standing in front of him. She walks across to the hob, turns it down a fraction, then continues across to him.

"Hello Jemma," he says eventually. Even her name is pretty, but you'd hardly think so the way it comes out of his mouth. She rises to kiss him on that mouth now, applying pressure but receiving none in return. He doesn't even put his arms around her, doesn't hold her the way he used to.

She pulls away from him and returns to the cooker. "Dinner won't be much longer. Why don't you sit down."

G786 takes a seat at the kitchen table and listens as Jemma makes small talk about her day, about the friends she's seen and the things she's done. None of it really interests him. Then, as she's serving up dinner, Jemma asks him how his own day has been—after all this time she still thinks he works for a finance company. He mumbles the usual "Fine," but doesn't go into any details. And while they eat she keeps looking at him, trying to find an answer, find some clues (she used to be able to tell what he was thinking by just looking at him, looking into his eyes . . . now she sees only a miniature reflection looking back). As usual, she wonders why he has gradually grown so distant, how the man she married could have become the person sitting there now. Had it been something she'd done? Had he gone off her? The fact that she couldn't bear him a child? Or maybe his love had just dwindled away, eroded over time . . .

That evening they watch the television; he has no preference. Doesn't laugh at the sitcoms anymore, doesn't cheer at the football or get passionate about the news reports. He just lets it all wash over him, and they sit there together on the couch like strangers, Jemma trying to snuggle up to him and getting nowhere. It's the same in bed. They undress, climb inside. She makes the first move, hoping against hope, but he presents his cold back to her. *Why doesn't he care anymore?* she wonders. If only he'd care . . . If only he'd . . . love her. Instead he sleeps, a mechanical action—a robot recharging. Jemma herself lies awake for hours, worrying about what has happened to her marriage, and what might happen in the future.

One thing is for sure, they cannot carry on like this forever.

*

In fact they only have to carry on like this for another two weeks.

G786 reports to the office on a Thursday morning this time. He is assigned one mission (the assassination of a scientist about to uncover a secret that might mean the end of civilisation as we know it—being as it's such a civilised world to begin with) before the alarms go off.

There are only two observers in his office today for a change, a puffy-faced man with triangular shoulders and a slender woman with long, blonde hair, and they both rush out into the corridor. G786 follows, but more slowly. They all believe there has been some sort of attack on the building; that some intelligence somewhere has discovered its true nature and detonated a bomb. As it turns out the wailing throb of the siren is simply an ordinary fire alarm. A soon-to-be *very* ex-employee had thrown a cigarette into a wastepaper bin in one of the downstairs offices without checking whether it was properly out (the offices are meant to be a non-smoking environment anyway, so this was his first mistake). The cigarette sets fire to the rubbish inside, which in turn sets fire to a desk beside it and the carpet on which it rests.

After the local smoke alarm went off, somebody smashed the larger fire alarm on the wall and it is this that's causing the panic. The sprinklers come on eventually. The standard procedure in any emergency is to get out and ask questions later, so this is what occurs. G786 and his supervisors do not risk the lifts. Instead they join a group of other workers making their way down the stairs. None of G786's fellow numbers are panicking as such . . . Only their observers.

They make it outside safely and stand around in the car park, unsure of what to do next. It takes twenty minutes for the cause of the accident to be discovered and dealt with by internal security (there is no way the proper authorities can be alerted—who knows what they might see inside there). The culprit is identified not long afterwards and detained, but the powers that be decide that all other staff might as well take the rest of the day off and return in the morning fresh. This will give security time to make doubly sure the building is safe and fit for the "workers".

This is how G786 comes to be driving home at such an early hour on a Thursday afternoon. He takes the same route as always, and makes very good time because there isn't much traffic at all. He uses the remote and parks his car in the garage, then enters his house through the kitchen door again. The kitchen is empty this time. He walks through into the hall and then checks the living-room. Jemma is not there. G786 doesn't call out; he simply goes upstairs to use the toilet. While he's up there he'll probably check to see if his wife is around. She isn't in either of the bedrooms or the study. He uses the toilet and flushes.

G786 knows that Jemma sometimes goes out in the day. He doesn't know where, because he doesn't really listen when she tells him things. To a friend's house probably or shopping . . . He doesn't care. Or at least he shouldn't. Except it's strange to return home and not find her here. Every day since they'd been married she'd been there to greet him when he walked through that kitchen door. Back when they'd first started living together, he used to sweep her up in his arms and kiss every available inch of her face. Why is he thinking about that now? He doesn't usually (he shouldn't). Could it be that . . . that he misses her being here? That emotions he'd thought he'd suppressed, that he thought had been driven out of him by months and months of doing what he now did, were actually still there. And had been all along . . .

He shook his head. You couldn't afford to think, to feel. To care. Not when you ended people's lives for a living. Not when you were a number rather than a name. A tool rather than a man. A weapon . . .

On his way back to the stairs he finds himself pausing outside the bedroom they share. He enters this again. What, is he tired? Does he need to lie down? No. G786 walks around the bed, as if he's never seen it before. It is a bed they sleep in together, inches apart and yet it might as well been miles—the miles he travels to take out a . . .

On the bedside table, on Jemma's side: a photograph he hasn't looked at in along time (he's tried not to). Their wedding day. G786 and Jemma smiling, laughing, as the crowd throws confetti on them. He knows that he was there that day, but it still seems like another man's memory. And actually it *is* another man's memory, isn't it? Simon's. G786 goes over to the picture, touches the frame with his fingers, touches the glass. Hopes that just as he can travel distances, he might somehow also be able to travel through time. Back to that day, to experience it all over again, just to remember what it felt like-

Why? Why bother? What was the point? What would it achieve? It certainly wouldn't alter his reality.

But it is too late. He needs to see Jemma now, if only for his own sake. *She'll be back soon,* he tells himself. Then he can see her all he wants. That's not the same though, she'll be here with him. It was never the same when she was here. G786 just needs to look upon her face without her knowing. It is a bizarre thing to admit, but true. And he can't explain it either, nor why he is now going to the window to close the curtains, going over to the wardrobe to get something out . . . a piece of her clothing, a dress, a skirt, a blouse . . . a jumper. One of her favourite fluffy jumpers. She wears this all the time when the cold weather's here. G786 grabs hold of it and sits back down on the bed.

He concentrates, rubbing the material between his thumb and fingers. G786 closes his eyes and enters the rainbow tunnel, the bright multi-coloured conduit. He zips up "roads", turns off junctions; but doesn't have to go that far this time. His wife is not in another country or on the other side of the world. She is in the next town. He arrives outside a building, tall and brown, doesn't really recognise the place but knows she is inside. He senses her. It's strange, but G786 thinks little of it. He just enters via the nearest wall, passing through bricks and mortar like a ghost. And enters a wide-open space with a counter on one side and a set of stairs on the other.

Ignoring the rest of it, he travels up these stairs without ever having to touch one of them. He flies, up through level after level, up and down corridor after corridor. Until at last he comes to a door. It's one of many, but it's the only one he sees. There is a number on the outside, very much like the one on his office door at work—except this one says 505. And it's a room rather than a person-number.

G786 passes through it.

Once inside, he sees his wife. But wishes to God (if there is a God) that he couldn't. She is in a room, in a bed. And she is not alone. A man, G786 doesn't recognise him, is on top of her. The sheets that cover the bottom half of his body are rising with him. Slowly, gently, tenderly. Jemma's hands are clutching his back, stroking the skin, digging her nails in as he speeds up. And now he is kissing her as he works, his lips brushing neck, and cheeks. Jemma's head flops to one side and G786 can see her face.

*What's the matter? You wanted to see her face, didn't you . . . ? Only not like this . . . Not like this . . .*

Jemma is in the throes of ecstasy, and G786 feels almost sick. A whirlwind of buried emotions are churning up inside him. Where before there was nothing (or almost nothing) he now feels love, jealously, anger, betrayal, hatred, and above all envy. Yes, envy. He, G786—Simon—wants to be in that bed with Jemma, as he once was, as he could have been all those many, many nights when he'd turned her away, ignored her, forced her to seek comfort in the arms of another. Forced her to find someone whom she *could* love and who would love her; give her what he could not. Warmth, humanity even.

It is too much for him to bear. No sooner has he thought about it, than he is there: inside the body of this stranger screwing his wife. Simon can feel the beating of the man's heart, faster and faster. How easy it would be to just squeeze that muscle until it burst. But he isn't going to do that. He has other things in mind.

Jemma looks up at the slick, rugged face above her. She's never felt so alive in her life—well, not since her and Simon used to . . . But suddenly something is wrong with the picture. Will—for that is the name of the man she finally gave herself to after months of resisting—is grimacing. Not because he is about to finish, but because of something else. His sweet, handsome face is swelling up. Forehead bloating, eyes bulging. And now his body is following suit. Shoulders inflating and skin stretching taut.

He rolls away and gets up off the bed. She watches as he staggers about there, clutching at his head, his chest, his whole torso in fact; not knowing where to put his hands first, or what help they could possibly be when they got there. A trickle of blood is running from the corner of his mouth now, then another down his nose. He begins to convulse, crying out in agony as spasms plague his now unrecognisable body.

It is only after Will explodes that Jemma starts to scream. Bits of him now adorn the walls, the furniture, and her. Free of the stranger, Simon looks down at his wife. The woman he loved, splattered in redness and screaming. He has done that, and he will do more besides. For he is not really a person at all, is he? He is a number, a tool, a weapon. And this is what he does . . .

*

Monday morning. G786 called in sick for the last day of the previous week, but he is back at work now. He drives to the offices in his car and parks it in the car park. He takes the lift and walks down the corridor to his office.

Inside there are three people waiting. A small man with curly hair, a bearded man with large ears, and a woman with a long, pointed nose. They are his observers for the day. The man with large ears rises and points to the file at the front.

G786 sits down and examines the pictures inside. He doesn't really look at them, doesn't need to. Just needs a vague idea of the location—that and the piece of material at the back.

They give him time to look anyway, then the small man closes the blinds.

"When you're ready." says the man.

And he is ready now. Oh so ready . . .

They wait as G786 shuts his eyes and rubs the material. They wait for him to join them back in the real world again, for him to open his eyes, tell them the mission was a success. But all he says when he eventually returns is:

"It's done. It's done."

# YOU DO THE MATH

## BY GENE O'NEILL

*. . . And luck always runs out.*
*—THELMA AND LOUISE*

Lucas Stanton was a lucky young man.

A tall, raw-boned, twenty-one-year-old, he had a tanned complexion, heavy-stubbled face even an hour after shaving, and rather non-descript, dead-pan features, people often saying he reminded them a little of Harry Dean Stanton; then they would quickly add, "Oh, but a younger version of course." Hardly shy and opinionated, he frequently interrupted conversations, and had the equally annoying habit of getting too close when he talked, invading other people's spaces. This lack of social grace, combined with a high-strung temperament, resulted in a number of verbal confrontations with colleagues that often left Lucas isolated and nursing a beat-up psyche. Fortunately for him, he was employed as a junior programmer at B of *A Headquarters*, able to retreat to his workstation, where he found the symbols on his PC screen ice for his bruised soul. As might be guessed, in attire and personal habits, he was compulsively neat—a trait that endeared him to his mother back in Cedar Rapids, but made zero impact otherwise, because Lucas had no male friends, even fewer of the feminine nomenclature. Since coming to San Francisco a year ago, he'd gone out on a grand total of one date, arranged by a desperate female programmer, who had an unattached roommate with a great personality. Of course the rather plain friend had even less social grace than Lucas, and the tense, ill-fated date ended up as an early evening fiasco.

But eight weeks ago, fate intervened, and Lucas's miserable social situation, including his love life, changed dramatically.

Finding his apartment near Nob Hill too expensive for his single salary after a third consecutive male roommate abruptly moved out, Lucas answered an ad in the *Chronicle*; and shortly thereafter he moved into a more modest, second floor, two bedroom flat off Divisidero Street near *Brother-in-laws #2*—the best rib takeout in the entire city— with two stunningly-gorgeous roommates.

Kat Vanderwaal was fair-skinned, her blonde hair spiked short; and like the words in the Beastie Boy's song, "Georgie's Girl," she had the Kip, the Pop, and the Pow—the kind of female passer-by on Montgomery Street described by Lucas's male colleagues as: "Your basic loaded-rack, thin-waisted, sweet-bootied heart-breaker." With her rosy cheeks and outdoor-girl look, she might have been a down-hill skier or skater on the US Olympic team . . . except Kat preferred indoor sports.

Exotic Gina Brown, with a Black father and Korean mother, had a tall, runner's body with gently-contoured curves, shoulder-length black hair, high cheek bones, almond-shaped ebony eyes, and wrinkle-free, smooth, coffee-coloured—just a dab of cream—skin. Her self-possessed, confident air discouraged any of the brothers—often kicking on Divisidero around the barbecue joint—from hitting on her when she passed by, most just appreciatively nodding their heads and declaring among themselves, "Oooh-whee, check out tha' foxy-lookin' mama."

Both women, mid-thirtyish, had recently gone through messy divorces and were currently unencumbered with significant-other attachments. They worked downtown as servers in the restaurant at *Nieman and Marcus*, were bright, well-read, enjoyed blues and jazz, ignored Lucas's lack of social skills, and praised him enthusiastically for his tidiness—of course he began doing housework on day one. The two older women probably thought of the awkward, young fellow as the team mascot, cuddly and safe—big mistake.

So, Lucas had indeed hit it lucky, because he soon found himself loving both of these gorgeous roommates—oh, no, not in any boring, chaste, platonic sense, uh-uh, but in the exciting, hardcore

Biblical way. It quickly developed into an adolescent male sexual fantasy, a living wet dream, a once in a lifetime erotic trip, better than any sleazy porno novel, an XXX rated . . . well, you do the math.

The sex began two nights after Lucas first moved into the flat and settled down on the hide-a-bed couch screened-off in the big living room, his stuff already stored neatly in the pair of corner amoires. He had slipped into his Simpson pyjamas and was stretched out on the hide-a-bed, just drifting in the twilight zone, when he heard a soft whisper from behind the screen.

"Luke, Luke . . . ?"

It was Kat, wearing a little-girl-scared expression and a big-girl, mauve, see-through, shortie, nightgown from *Victoria's Secret*, nothing visible underneath except her kip, pop, pow.

"I had a bad nightmare," she explained in a barely audible, frightened voice to Lucas, who couldn't help staring at her enticingly full breasts with large aureoles and nipples. "And I can't go back to sleep. Would you do me a little favour, Luke, Sweety-pie?"

"S-s-sure," he stammered back, unable to keep his gaze from sliding down to her silky pubic triangle, the pale colour matching her spiked hair.

Kat firmly took his hand in hers, tugging him up from his bed. "Come into my bedroom and lie down with me until I go to sleep. Just for a few minutes, okay?"

He nodded, too choked up to even grunt an affirmative reply, and awkwardly tiptoed after her into the master bedroom. She carefully eased the door closed behind them.

At her bedside, Lucas remained standing stiffly, not really knowing what was expected of him.

Kat stood in front of the gangly young man, her eyes not at all fearful now. In fact her lids drooped in a kind of sexy manner.

"I usually sleep in the buff," she announced, her husky tone matching her seductive expression. She slipped out of the flimsy shortie and moved closer, kissing Lucas wetly, her tongue tracing his lips in a clockwise pattern

"How about you, Luke?" Kat finally asked, sitting down on the bed in front of him, and gently pulling down his pyjama bottoms. "Did I ever tell you that you remind me of Harry Dean Stanton? I just love his movies, you know."

This isn't really happening, he thought, closing his eyes, unable to say anything at all for fear of stammering stupidly and breaking the spell.

But it was happening.

In a few seconds Kat coaxed Lucas to full arousal where he stood, using the same clockwise tracing manoeuvre with her tongue. Then, she retrieved a condom from under her pillow and deftly rolled it onto his erect penis. She pushed him down on his back, telling him, "You just let Mama take care of everything, Sweety-pie." Without any more foreplay, she easily mounted Lucas, pressed his shoulders flat, and rode him hard, whispering in his ear, "This quickie's for you, Luke." And the frantic ride was indeed over shortly, both of them sitting up, their nakedness slick with sweat.

"Now," Kat purred after a few minutes rest, "my turn."

Then, the older woman proceeded to instruct the younger man in some of the finer points of female anatomy and physiology—details somehow not covered in Human Biology 101 back at Iowa City. This course was followed by a little slippery lab work in

Oral-Genital Applications 501.

Shortly before dawn, Kat took an exhausted Lucas by the hand, scooped up his pyjamas, and led him back to his bed in the frontroom.

"Thanks, Luke, you're a darling," she whispered, smiling gratefully. "I'm really not frightened anymore." Taking a step around his screen, she murmured over her shoulder, "I think I'll be able to sleep just fine, now.

*

Groggy but intellectually enriched by the grand instructional experience, Lucas just nodded at the screen, and whispered back, in a tired voice, "Sweet dreams, Kat."

Late the next night, Wednesday, a very different but equally educational scenario was repeated in the other bedroom with Gina. The dark-skinned beauty was an equally adept instructor, covering the high points of Human Sexuality 101, 201, 301 . . . Oh well, you do the math.

Stumbling back into his frontroom bed early Thursday morning,

Lucas had enough remaining strength to just whisper a post-course, positive evaluation to himself: "Holy Microsoft, dude, you've died and gone to heaven!"

Then, Friday night about 10:00 p.m. Lucas was called into Kat's candle-lit master bedroom, where he heard Bill Withers softly singing the blues—"Ain't No Sunshine When She's Gone"—and saw a bottle of Napa Valley Cabernet Sauvignon, three wine glasses, some kind of bottled lotion or scented oil, and a half-dozen rolled joints—Humbolt Indica?—on a serving tray on the nightstand. Sitting lotus fashion on the bed were Gina and Kat, their eyes heavy-lidded, chanting the Tibetan mantra, "Ooommm, ma-ni, pay-me, hoommm," and looking lovely, sexy, and totally zen-like in their bare-assed kips, pops, pows.

"Ah, the young and eager grasshopper," Kat said, her words slightly slurred but professorial in manner.

"Luke, hon," Gina said, smiling seductively and beckoning him to join them, "welcome to Zanadu."

He shucked his clothes and did join them . . . with enthusiasm.

And that was the first of their weekly Friday-night all-skates, a sweaty, slippery, moaning, world-class rasslin event that Lucas couldn't even accurately describe, much less imagine in his wildest sexual fantasies.

He was indeed a lucky young man, despite his resemblance to Harry Dean Stanton, temperament, and complete lack of social skills.

But even Eden had a minor glitch that generated major problems for the inhabitants. Likewise here at the second-story classroom, lab, and rasslin ring just off Divisidero Street near *Brother-in-laws #2*.

Lucas soon discovered both of his older roommates were terrible slobs: They left dirty dishes stacked in the sink, covered every horizontal surface in the apartment with glasses, cups, and plates; night-after-night he found discarded clothes everywhere, once a pair of dirty sky-blue panties showed up in an unfilled ice tray in the fridge; and neither woman had apparently ever developed a close working relationship with dish towels, scrub brushes, *Comet*, the *Hoover*, or dusting cloths—even when it came to their own bedrooms. So, Lucas dutifully did all picking-up, cleaning, dishwashing, laundering, and even regularly changed the sheets in both bedrooms when he changed his own on the hide-a-bed. But over the course of eight weeks the appearance of the constantly trashed apartment and the inefficient division of labour ground on his compulsively-neat psyche, fraying his already tightly-wound nerves.

By the time all six junior programmers were laid off when B of A moved its headquarters east, Lucas had developed an assortment of tics and twinges, accompanied with a host of ritual-like mannerisms of an extreme obsessive-compulsive, like the romance writer in *As Good As It Gets*.

In a word, Lucas Stanton was a psychological mess.

Thursday night, after cleaning the toilet seat and sink before washing his hands thoroughly, Lucas finally sat down and just began to relax when he spotted the last straw and gasped with disbelief. It was a used *Kotex* sitting on the edge of the bathtub—not in the trash or even rolled up, but in blatant full view.

His pulse raced, his heart thudded wildly, his chest tightened, and he gagged on the sour juices flooding his mouth. Jumping up, Lucas turned and vomited into the toilet. Then, pulling up his pants, he stumbled into the frontroom but froze in place . . . something really weird happening inside of him. It was like his frayed nerves were a mass of rubber bands holding his psyche together, but stretched too tightly for too long; and eventually reaching critical mass, they individually began snapping apart, each internal cerebral *ping* sending a painful shock wave rippling across his synapses. Lucas finally howled with the agony of it, sending his startled roommates scurrying for cover.

Then he convulsed and blacked out . . .

When Lucas came to his senses, both bedroom doors were closed, the flat dead quiet. He felt oddly divorced from himself, separated from reality, almost like he was watching a double of himself in a movie, everything that happened was happening to someone else. Looking about, he realised it was quite late; and he was tired. Uncharacteristically, Lucas didn't pick up the nightly mess before retiring; instead, he just flopped down on the couch and dropped off into a deep sleep.

Late Friday morning, Lucas awakened to the enticing smells of breakfast cooking in the kitchen—coffee, bacon . . . something baking?

Kat came out from the kitchen. "I'm sorry about the sanitary napkin last night, Luke—"

Her eyes widened with an incredulous look.

"Lucas Stanton!" she said in an accusatory voice.

"What, what—?"

He looked around under the cover that was tangled around him, expecting to find a strange person sleeping beside him.

"You didn't wear your Simpsons or even pull out the hide-a-bed," Kat said, as if lecturing a ten-year-old. "You slept fully dressed with your shoes on. That's so, so . . . unlike you. And look what you've done to the couch."

He stood up, dragging the cover with him. There were dark scuff-marks from his shoes all over the back and arm in the corner of the white cotton couch. "Jesus," he swore with no real affect, like he was speaking a line automatically in a dull play.

Kat was shaking her head sadly. "That couch and bed cost Gina $1500 on sale. Man, when she sees this you are going to be in deep doo doo!"

He reached down with his tee shirt and tried to wipe off the scuffmarks. No luck. All he did was smudge them slightly. It would probably require some professional cleaning; but he'd take care of it. No reason for Kat to go off on it.

In fact, he couldn't quite believe this scenario, Kat in a kind of Martha Stewart, super-homemaker mode. Maybe he was dreaming or in a drug flashback to his high school days in Cedar Rapids, actually being lectured by his mother. Could smoking too much dope do that? He wasn't sure. All he knew was he felt abnormally relaxed, but still kind of divorced from it all.

"Hey, chill out," Lucas finally murmured to Kat or whoever was ranting at him, with a shrug and fake apologetic smile.

"Chill out? I'll fucking chill out."

The blonde woman in front of him was enraged.

Her look activated a rush of defensive adrenaline as Lucas struggled to his feet, causing the few remaining intact rubber bands to ping apart in his skull. His vision blurred from the sudden pain.

"I'm going to get Gina up for breakfast and tell her just what the fuck you've done—"

"No," he ordered, grabbing the woman's arm, his pulse racing wildly now, his voice sounding like someone else, a distant echo in a tunnel. "You're not going to tell anyone anything."

She jerked out of his grasp, her China-blue eyes flashing. "Oh, yes, I am. And this just might be it for me, buster. You've been an unbearable asshole since the lay-off, you know that? Maybe we all need to talk about you hunting for a new place."

No longer emotionally detached, Lucas felt the pressure building inside him, and a roaring in his ears blocked out the older woman's carping voice. Then his vision tunnelled as the cold rage inside claimed him . . .

Later that evening, Lucas woke up naked in the master bedroom with Kat beside him. She too was lying naked on the bed, so beautiful . . . except for some ugly tattoos on her throat—funny indigo marks. In a kind of confused state, he stumbled into the bathroom, found Kat's facial blush and a dusting pad. He covered the marks as best he could with the make-up, then gently arranged her head on the pillow. Ah, that looked much better, he thought, still fighting to pull himself together. She was so beautiful and so quiet now. She needs her rest, he thought, remembering it was almost time for their Friday night all-skate. He'd go next door and get Gina.

Lucas rapped lightly on the other bedroom door, and entered the darkened room, waiting a moment for his eyes to adjust to the dimness. Gina was apparently asleep, resting on her side, her ebony hair fanned out in back of her on the pillow.

He crawled into bed beside her, just the touch of her bare breasts against his chest exciting him. "It's almost ten o'clock," he whispered, reaching down and gently caressing her furry sex. He groaned, fully aroused now. Snuggling closer, her skin felt odd, cold and clammy to his touch; and when he tried to kiss her, her unresponsive lips were icy. He stared dumbfounded for a moment into Gina's dully-glazed eyes. Only then did he really notice the indigo tattoos on the dark skin of her neck, similar to Kat's. But the coincidence made no impact on his dazed confusion.

Knowing Gina wouldn't want to miss out on tonight's rasslin match, he carried her into Kat's bedroom and stretched her out, resting her head on the other pillow. Just before he crawled into bed between the two women, he frowned, sniffing the air, noticing a mildly offensive aroma. He tried to file a mental note to look for some incense later, but he forgot it as soon as he took his place between his two gorgeous roommates, only remembering to breath through his mouth . . . Then, for just a brief moment an ugly thought surfaced in his confused mental fog: *Something terrible has happened here; you've done something very bad.* But the thought quickly dropped back into the murk, not really having any impact on his behaviour. For he felt a tightening in his groin, a growing sexual excitement, as he remembered it was time for their weekly all-skate.

Lucas grinned with lascivious anticipation.

*

Three days later, after a half-dozen concerned phone calls from the *Nieman Marcus* restaurant, the landlady discovered the three of them in the vile-smelling flat, still lying on the king-size in the master bedroom—only the man in the middle alive, but in a dehydrated stupor, babbling incoherently about skating or something.

For Lucas Stanton luck had just run out.

You do the math.

# OF KINGS AND WORMS

## BY JOHN URBANCIK

You think your dreams are just that: images and visions thrown haphazardly together by an unwinding mind. And maybe, sometimes, that's all dreams are.

But think carefully. Look back at your night-time adventures. There have been those few that stick with you, so much so that you still smell something, upon waking, that never existed. Or an image returns, vivid and detailed, the moment your eyelids close.

Those are the types of dreams I'm talking about. I don't know anything about the ones you can't remember. Maybe that's your future self trying to warn you of something. I know I'm trying.

One night—I can't rightly say how long ago, since time functions differently in the realm of dreams—a bunch of us went to sleep. Maybe you did, too. And maybe you even saw some of what I'm about to tell you. This night, one dream overrode all others. Even my father was there, dreaming, though he'd been dead a couple of years already. Like I said, time doesn't work the same.

The Queen of Dreams, a pretty black woman with a purple robe, addressed us. "It's time to choose a partner. Someone to rule beside me. Someone who can face up to the Nightmare Demons of the Western Realms and not soil his pants. If you think you're the one, just reach out, touch the orb in front of you." Turning, she added, "There will be a test."

Tentatively, I extended my hand. Dozens around me did, also. I don't remember seeing you, but maybe you thought about it. Most of us, I think, almost surrendered blindly to this.

Not everyone. Some shrank away from these floating orbs—pink things which appeared as touchable as anything from a fabric softener commercial. They were convinced, and I nearly joined them, that someone else would touch the orb and prevent them from having to do so.

"Reach farther," they said, and one of us did. Not just any one: me.

I didn't do it alone. Dozens of us touched the pink globes simultaneously. The majority, fearing the thing, were left behind.

Touching the balls, which no longer existed, transported us to another section of the Dream World. Here, we intrepid souls stood together to face the test. Only the one who would be King, we knew, would escape this place.

I don't know what demons anyone else faced. I heard one guy scream, and knew by the smell that he'd failed in the queen's challenge. A woman near me flailed her arms, swatting at something I couldn't see.

I expected the worst.

The worst came: I doubled over, my stomach twisting in sudden agony, and expelled a worm through my mouth. Then another. These were not your average earthworms; they were huge, growing even as they escaped my body.

And growing, they turned on me. Rows of tiny teeth lined their huge mouths—maws large enough to swallow me whole, as if I were a snake's guinea pig.

I stood my ground. Maybe that was my mistake. But the Dream Queen had only said we needed to face our nightmares, not defeat them. The first of the worms enveloped me. Its teeth—razors—scratched my skin. I struggled, earning more scrapes on my arms and legs.

The worm's body was translucent. My vision wasn't perfect, but it became quickly apparent that the other worms were going to fight over me.

And I wasn't done throwing them up. Another worm wriggled out of my throat. And another. And another.

I don't know who overcame their nightmare. I don't even know if the Dream Queen found her King. After what might have been days, years, or merely moments, I saw my chance and escaped the fighting worms.

I still throw them up every so often—even in the waking world, because I never really returned. I've seen my grave. They told me it was a lovely service.

Ugh . . . there's that feeling again, like something's crawling around the insides of my stomach. Did you think those were butterflies?

# BLUE MOON SONATA

## BY GEORGE IVANOFF

"Oh . . . they exist. Just like you and I. Not necessarily in the way popular mythology portrays them . . . but they do very much exist. Most people just don't realise it." Professor Boadicea paused, as if struck by some new profound truth. "Or perhaps . . . they choose not to realise it. The human mind is capable of convincing itself of almost anything, despite evidence to the contrary."

She leaned back in her chair, the leather creaking as she moved, and ran the long, immaculately manicured nail of her right index finger across her lips. She stared across her cluttered desk and allowed herself a brief smile. "That's why you're so special . . . you choose not to ignore the signs."

Friederic nodded warily. He didn't quite know how to react to the Professor and her revelations. He stared at her face—striking, beautiful even, despite the crawling advance of wrinkled age. How old was she? At least 60. It was the eyes that did it, he thought. They created the intrigue. Open, yet veiled. Filled with a subdued, wild energy. The windows to her soul. As always, the curtains were drawn, although not quite meeting, allowing a tantilising glimpse of what lay inside—a hint of things to come, perhaps.

The lack of conversation pervaded the room. Hung around them. Making their breathing almost deafeningly loud. The Professor rasped in and out with short, furtive breaths. Friederic's were long and slow in an attempt to control his racing heart.

*What does she expect me to say,* Friederic wondered.

"So . . ." he began tentatively, "you approve of the topic?"

In a quick, fluid motion that seemed completely unhurried, the Professor leaned forward, extracted a spiral bound, plastic covered, sheaf of paper and tossed it across her desk. It landed face down in front of Friederic, teetering precariously on the edge of the desk, ready at any moment to plunge forward onto the floor.

"Oh, I more than approve of the topic . . . I applaud it." Her eyes met Friederic's and held them in a vice-like grip. "An inspired topic, a well-presented argument and approach, and a comprehensive bibliography." He couldn't tear his gaze away. "The Faculty will undoubtedly try not to approve it . . . " She smiled again, although this time it lingered at the corners of her mouth as if in anticipation of some long-desired passion. "But I can handle them."

Friederic breathed a silent sigh of relief as she released his eyes in order to glance out the window. "But of course there are things you haven't taken into account." As she stared out across the campus, the silence stretched. After a while, he noticed that the Professor's hand was moving—just slightly, almost imperceptibly, but moving nonetheless. It was a delicate, rhythmic motion, as if she were keeping time to some secret melody that no one else could hear.

"Need!" she finally announced, her voice startling Friederic as it dismembered the silence. Her hand stilled, but she continued to stare out the window. "A need has been overlooked. But, being a proposal, it's not yet a serious oversight." She continued to look out of the window, her gaze drifting across buildings and grounds—a bizarre juxtaposition of architectural styles, the contemporary alongside the archaic, the aesthetic with the utilitarian, the real and the mythic, the lyrical, the tuneless.

"I think we should discuss it further."

She looked back across the desk, her eyes seeking to meet his again. Friederic avoided them, looking down, instead, at his proposal, still balanced on the precipice, neither safe nor in real danger.

"Come back after sunset!"

Friederic's heart thudded hard in his chest and he looked up suddenly, eyes wide, to find that Professor Boadicea had turned her back on him again. She had swiveled her chair around to face the large, sealed window. None of the windows above the second floor in any of the university buildings could be opened. They had all been sealed for the protection of the students, years ago after a brief spate of suicides.

Friederic's mind raced through the possibilities, trying to formulate an acceptable, convincing excuse.

"I . . ."

"After sunset," insisted the Professor as if anticipating his response. "I'm sure you can manage that . . . if you want your topic approved." Silence for a while, then she raised her hand in a dismissive wave, still not turning around.

Friederic stood up to leave, catching his proposal as it finally fell off the edge. As he left the office, he noticed the calendar on the wall beside the door, with today's date circled in red.

*

Friederic sat quietly in *Bygone Daze*, a trendy on-campus cafe. As the grad students sipped at their cappuccinos, espressos and whatever version of the standard coffee happened to be popular that week, he stared at the thesis proposal in his hands.

He was beginning to think that this whole thing may have been a mistake, a lapse in judgement on his part. Right from the start he had realised that the topic would be a risk, but . . .

Wanting to see him after sunset on this particular day couldn't be a coincidence—the mark on her calendar attested to that. She knew! And she must have a purpose. She always had a purpose in other things—why should this be any different. The Professor was a formidable academic, he'd always known that, from the first moment he had walked into her cultural anthropology class as an undergraduate—but now he was beginning to sense something more. What? Evil? No. Power? Maybe. Determination? Yes! Yes, there was determination in those eyes, in the way she held herself . . . but there was more to it than that. There was . . . the feeling—no, the certainty—that there was something hidden. Something below the surface, unseen yet undeniably there.

Friederic smiled as his mind created the image of Professor Boadicea as an iceberg in the ocean of academia, ramming ships with words such as STUDENTS, ADMINISTRATION and THE FACULTY OF ARTS emblazoned on their sinking hulls.

"Vienna Mocha?"

Friederic, startled out of his reverie, almost flew from his seat. His muscles tense and ready for action, he calmed himself and nodded to the waitress. As she placed the coffee on the table and glided away, he made a mental note that he would have to work on being less jumpy. Any lapse in control was a potential risk.

Looking down at his coffee he was dismayed to discover it had been served in a glass rather than a cup or mug. Although he had been hanging out in *Bygone Daze* since his freshman year, much to the annoyance of some of the snobbier postgrads, he still hadn't quite figured out their system for which types of coffee were served in what sort of receptacle. It didn't help that it seemed to change from week to week, from waitress to waiter.

He sighed as he folded up the paper serviette and tried using it to pick up the glass without burning his fingers. He almost had the glass to his lips, when the serviette slipped. Coffee sloshed across the table-top and over his thesis proposal. Grabbing another serviette he proceeded to mop the coffee from the plastic cover until the title could again be seen.

*The Cultural significance of Lunar Images in Popular Mythology and its Relationship to Subliminal Lycanthropy: a comparative analysis of oral history, literature and the visual media.*

*

Friederic could hear the music as he approached the door. It was vaguely familiar, yet he couldn't quite place it. He paused without knocking, allowing the music to carry him off with it. The lyrical strains of the violin were gentle and playful as they raced along the scales. Friederic found then enticing, vaguely sensual. As the piano accompaniment began, the violin slowly changed. The sounds transformed from melodic to harsh. Jarring notes that seemed not to fit, that were somehow wrong and out-of-place, yet at the same time almost expected. The piano became quiet and distant, drowned out by the string instrument. Soon, after a final spasmodic collection of notes, it stopped altogether and the violin changed yet again. Triumph! There was triumph in those sounds.

"Well, are you going to come in?"

The Professor was looking out through the opened door. Friederic had been so engrossed in the music he hadn't noticed her opening it. The image of the iceberg returned briefly and he almost laughed. But he stopped himself in time, looking down at his own feet.

He nodded, embarrassed, and entered the office, avoiding the Professor's eyes. He felt her hand brush his shoulder as he walked by her, and shivered.

Inside, he was hit with the full force of the music. It was triumph, he realised, but more. Glee? Amusement? Gloating!

He was about to ask what the piece was, when abruptly it ceased, as if its life had suddenly ended.

"Music!" the Professor announced, touching his shoulder again as she walked around him to settle herself in the chair behind her desk. "That is what you lack."

"I beg your pardon?"

"Your thesis proposal," she explained. "There is no mention of music."

Friederic opened his mouth to reply, but the Professor continued.

"Music is an incredibly powerful cultural force. It is influenced . . . shaped by popular culture. And in turn, that culture is also influenced and shaped by the music. Down through the ages it has been so."

*Oh no*, thought Friederic, *she's in lecture mode.*

"As soon as the human race started to form music, it became the accompaniment to their dreams, their fears and their actions. People listen to it for entertainment, relaxation, inspiration, enlightenment, direction . . . the reasons are as endless as diversity of mind. People have sung to it, slept to it, worked to it, made love to it, killed and maimed to it . . . committed unspeakable acts while it played on."

She picked up a remote control and pressed a button with the tip of a lacquered nail. Were they longer than they had been earlier in the day? Friederic wondered. Longer? Darker?

Friederic nearly jumped out of his seat, the volume was so loud.

A 1950s doo-wop version of *Blue Moon* assaulted the room, played through unseen speakers.

Professor Boadicea turned to look out her window and pressed the remote again.

The music abruptly changed. *Bad Moon Rising.* Still just as loud.

She stared out at the night campus, awash with alternating dim, bright and indifferent lights and intellects. Nameless, faceless people moved about below—oblivious shadows in the semi-darkness. The sky was brooding, clouded over.

Friederic's attention focused momentarily on the window. *Sealed*, he thought, nodding to himself.

Again, the Professor's nail on the remote.

"By the light, of the silvery moon," a voice he didn't recognise sang briefly before being cut off.

Remote.

A piece of classical music he didn't know the name of.

Remote.

*Moonlight Serenade?* He wasn't sure.

Remote.

Then several pieces in quick succession, with barely enough notes to make then recognisable, finishing with a song he did know.

"And if your head explodes with dark forbodings too

I'll see you on the dark side of the moon."

The lyrics sidled up to him suggestively.

Then the Professor turned the volume down, allowing her voice some space in the room.

"I could go on all night . . . but I assume you get the point."

"You want me to . . . "

"Not want . . . *need*."

After some time, the song finished and then they sat in silence for a while.

"You *need* the music, Friederic. I *need* the music."

Silence again.

"It's the soundtrack for what's about to be played out."

More silence.

"There's a full moon tonight," she finally said, still looking out of the window, searching the sky.

"Yes. I know," said Friederic. "I wondered about you choosing this night."

The Professor chuckled to herself.

"I didn't choose it . . . it chose me."

"Yes."

As if on cue, the sky grew gracious—the clouds parted a little and the moon made a partial appearance. The professor fumbled with the remote. "I need . . . "

The music started again. The same music Friederic had arrived to. As she continued to gaze out the window, her hand began to conduct the music, the remote her baton.

"What is this piece?"

"Once of my own compositions," she answered, turning up the volume. "It's called *Blue Moon Sonata*."

"It's an intriguing piece." Friederic raised an eyebrow. "I didn't realise you were . . . a musician."

"Not in any formal sense. I dabble as part of my research." She chuckled again. "An anthropological musician. Not at all proficient."

"Which instrument do you play?'

"Pardon?"

"Violin or piano?" he insisted.

"Does it matter?" She turned the music up even more. "So long as the music is played."

"Do you play often?" Friederic's voice was barely audible over the sonata.

As the piano accompaniment began, the clouds seemed to disperse before their eyes.

The Professor turned slightly. Just enough to see Friederic but to still gaze out at the night . . . just enough for him to catch a glimpse of light in her eye. Big and fat, seemingly filling the entire sky, the overpowering icon was reflected in her gaze.

"Once in a blue moon," she smiled.

Then, as she got up out of her chair and turned, Professor Boadicea saw the same light in Friederic's eyes.

The music reached crescendo.

# THE DREAM QUEEN

## BY M.J. MURPHY

He found Alexus at Bunny's, a strip club up in Newmarket, along the East edge of town where the truckers and the bikers spent their paycheques to stare at girls strip naked to rock-n-roll music from the 1970s. Alexus was new to the place, a little blonde, bubble-gum creature, with a chest straight out of a comic book. Her breasts were two warm, mothering eyes around a tiny mouth that was her belly button. They defined her, like another girl's red hair or freckles might define them.

Alexus shook it to Led Zeppelin. She began the act wearing $8 track pants, a L.A. Raiders jersey, and hippie sandals, which she removed at the rate of about one item per song. Alexus didn't have a lot of dancing talent. Her breasts swung pendulously and threatened to tip her over with every move. And she just stood there for about twenty seconds, fiddling with the drawstring on her pants, before she could get them off. But the guys loved her—the clumsy little girl with the big boobs. They identified with her in her awkwardness; their emotions were channelled through three hundred semi-erect peckers.

Alexus gave them the muff first (a perfect black triangle) and the ass second before she ditched the football jersey. And Lockridge had to laugh, because the girl was not without her cunning stratagems. Underneath was a white tank-top emblazoned with a Supergirl logo; it reached just past her nipples, covered just enough that she was not entirely exposed. Low howls rippled through the crowd at the sight.

And then the top came off, and there they were, natural wonders.

Alexus waved the perspiration soaked garment above her head like a trophy, then tossed it out over the tables. Two men fought for it. Other men waved money and pointed, and a bidding war broke out. Alexus was oblivious; she threw a pink towel down on the stage and rolled around naked with "Going to California" playing on the sound system, doing the obligatory "floor work to a ballad" that ended every act at Bunny's. Usually, the place calmed down during this final phase, and Lockridge might go back to reading his news-paper. This time however the boys stood and showered Alexus with money. Tables splintered as the fight continued. Eventually, the winner sold his prize to a third man for $300.

Alexus was Susan Gladly; she had to be. There was the same but-terfly tattoo on her left shoulder, the same Zep tunes, the cheap outfits she wore in all her routines.

But Susan had vanished 20 years ago; just not been there one day when he called by her apartment with flowers. Her clothes lay scat-tered over the furniture. The tv played "I Love Lucy". The police, when he summoned them, were stumped and not particularly inter-ested. There were no "clues" to be found, and she was a stripper . . .

Lockridge had convinced himself that Susan was the one, the world, for him. When they'd been going together he had tried to convince her to give up the club life; he intended to marry her, after all. And when she disappeared he had declared that part of his life over with. He would be done with relationships. Now he was 45 year old, a balding bachelor who had spent, when you calculated it all out, about the length of World War I in places like Bunny's.


Alexus passed his table, set in a dark corner against the wall, on her way to the girls' change-room. She was wrapped in her towel, like a candy stuck to pink wrapping paper.

"Susan!"

And she **looked** at him, as though they had once shared secrets. Then she was through the door. He glared at the bouncer standing guard, averted his eyes when Stanley glared back.

Another girl came onstage and stripped. Bill sat down again and drank. Time passed.

*

He smelled her nearby, and a hand landed on his shoulder. "Hey sailor!" And there she was; Susan Gladly, dressed in street clothes and fresh out of the shower. She was as blonde as a beach on a sunny day. "You look sooo familiar," she said, touching his shoulder like she owned him, like a wife. "Have we met?"

" . . . in many places," he replied smoothly. "I've chased you through the past and through the future and around all the stars in the galaxy. We've been meant for each other since before time began."

For a moment, Alexus stared at him like he had hit her with something. Then she giggled brightly, and the smoky club air around her glowed pale yellow. He told her this, and she blushed. The blush flowed red down her neck and under her top, until the air burned crimson.

They sat together, and he told her all sorts of other things.

"I love Italian," she replied.

He hated Italian food—what had he just said? "Well let's go then!"

"Whoa cowboy. My last set is in a couple of minutes."

"Did you say that already?"

"Only about TEN times."

"When you speak I hear music. Sometimes I miss the words."

She giggled again, blushed, slapped her hands over her cheeks. "I better go get changed. This set may go on a bit longer than normal. Someone may want to get spanked."

*

At Midnight they were huddled together over a Pizza at Julio's. He kept it up with the bad poetry, and Alexus thrilled to every stupid line. She would laugh at his jokes, too, even when he forgot how the ending went, just because she wanted them to be funny.

Later they took a cab to Alexus' room at the Everett and made love, many times, until they had rendered one another boneless and exhausted. They fell asleep entwined like the roots of two old oak-trees.

*

Bill Lockridge dreamt of a dark wood, of walking along a narrow path through the trees of this wood, where he came upon the figure of a sleeping woman. She was Alexus, but her skin in this place was transparent and a window into another world, where he could see yet another forest, even darker and utterly pathless. Bill Lockridge touched the girl and she popped like a soap bubble. He fell into the blank space within and discovered himself lying face-down upon wet grass. Rain pelted his cheeks and lightning flashed overhead. Something moved in the undergrowth, snuffling like a wild boar.

Lockridge awoke, soaked in a sweat that tasted like cold rain.

Alexus had escaped him. She lay over on the far side of the bed. Carefully, Lockridge took her around the waist and pulled her into him, until he had wrapped her body to his own like a blanket of warm, pale clay.

*

Lockridge took Alexus to Sunnybrook Park, where buskers played alongside the trails to small groups of Sunday wanderers, and little lambs nuzzled you at the petting zoo. He bought her cotton candy, which immediately found its way into her hair and over her t-shirt. Susan would have done exactly the same thing.

"I love being with you, baby, but you've got to stop calling me that name."

"But you remind me . . . "

"Forget her," Alexus said, sounding jealous. "Think of me and me alone. You promise to?"

"Sure."

They sat on the grass under a beechwood tree. The sun warmed her shoulders and he brushed her hair with his fingers. Later they wandered around the lake, feeding hotdog buns to the ducks.

*

Alexus had time off between engagements, so they spent it out and about the city. Over Bill's objections, Alexus insisted on paying for dinner, for the movie, for whatever. It turned out she was loaded, all of it stashed in a money belt and a pair of runners that came with a false sole.

"You've got to stop thinking of me as a helpless little girl, Bill. I make $1,000 a night when I'm working. And that's without fucking anyone."

"I hope they don't pay you in those," he said as she flipped through the bills she had pulled from her shoe.

One bill had a picture of an old man with a long white beard on it. "10 Cruzeiro. The Bank of Brazil."

"Its money somewhere, dear."

"In Brazil, dear. Where'd you get that?"

Alexus shrugged mysteriously. "Do I have enough of the real stuff?"

"More than enough"

"Then help me spend it, Bill, that's what you're supposed to do with money."

Back home at his apartment, where Alexus had been staying the past few days, Lockridge put Barry Manilow on the stereo and sat the girl on the edge of his bed. Though blonde, her lifestyle had made Alexus into a night creature, and she had burned in the sun. He rubbed Solarcane into her poor pretty shoulders.

"I guess I'll be okay," she said, like a half-naked bunny, two square, white teeth biting into her lower lip from the pain. "Tans enhance the undi-lines, and guys love to see white skin. White means forbidden."

"You are the love of my life," he said to her.

"Uh huh."

"We'll be together until we die."

She giggled. "At least until one of us does."

*

He dreamt that he was in pyjamas walking along some kind of rural road. His feet were naked, and the asphalt cold beneath. He could see lights ahead from the city of Hamilton. Its refinery smokestacks glowed yellow; their pale reflections glowed green on the waters of Lake Ontario.

Just down the road a Honda Civic struck an SUV and went sailing. It careened end-over-end into a farmer's field to his right, bouncing jauntily towards him, shedding chunks of glass and metal as it went.

The burning engine sparked white as it caught fire, dazzling and warming him as the wreck passed overhead.

And the SUV erupted into a flower of black and yellow. Something inside the cabin burned furiously, flapping what might have been an arm.

He stood in the middle of the road and watched.

By the time it rolled to a stop the roof of the Honda had been squashed flat to the body, and the flames from the SUV lit up the surrounding fields for a mile in every direction. There was no question of staging a rescue.

He wondered, abstractly, if his presence, the presence of a man in his pyjamas walking down the middle of a highway, had caused any of this.

A pickup truck approached along a dirt service side-road to the left, bumping up and down through the potholes. "Hello!" Lockridge hollered.

"You okay?" a man's voice called from inside of the cab.

He nodded. "I guess."

"What happened?"

"I don't know. I think I've been sleepwalking. "

*

Later, he sat cozy in the back of a police car, behind its two officers. He watched firetrucks hose down the SUV and the Honda. They burned stubbornly, so progress was slow.

A fist knocked on the window. The cops jumped in their seats, spilled their coffee.

"I brought the gentleman a coat ." It was the farmer, named Ted Braithewaite, who'd been driving the pickup truck.

The glass descended.

"You okay?" Ted asked, passing an old dufflecoat in. "You can have this."

"Thanks. Can I borrow your cell-phone?"

"You're not being charged with anything," said one of the cops.

"I need to call my girlfriend."

He let Braithewaite activate the cell for him, then dialed the number to his apartment. Alexus answered sleepily after the third ring. "Hello?" Her voice this late at night was five years old, timid and innocent.

"Honey, it's Bill, I need you to come pick me up. Bring my runners, please, and my wallet."

*

Alexus cried the whole way home. Lockridge, on the other hand, was philosophical. "I walk fifteen miles in my bare feet and there's not a scratch on them," he said as he drove. Alexus stared at him, tragedy brewing behind her eyes, but did not reply.

"Three people died right in front of me," he continued. "But I'm not traumatised. I wonder if I should feel like that?"

"You're in shock."

He shrugged. "Shock feels fine, then."

*

He phoned in sick and they played in his bed all day long. She pressed against him desperately, as though he might be lost to her if she couldn't sink her flesh into his. They bit and scratched at one another until the bedsheets were pink with blood. Later, as he lay in the bathtub, Alexus climbed him and licked his wounds. Her nipples dripped milk onto his chest as her head bobbed up and down. The day passed slowly and luxuriously.

By nine PM, Bill Lockridge was ready for sleep. He called to Alexus.

"Something on tv I wanna watch," she replied lazily from the living room. "I'll be along in a while."

He didn't have the strength to argue.

But he awoke cold. Alexus wasn't there and the clock radio read Midnight. Panicked, wrapped in a white sheet, Lockridge found her out in the living room asleep before the television set. "I Love Lucy" was playing on channel 3, the oldies network.

Calm again, Lockridge was content to simply watch Alexus for a time. It always amazed him how deeply the girl slept, as though she had died and her soul gone travelling in another world where she was the Queen.

Finally, he carried her to bed. She seemed light as an angel.

*

His right arm went numb. He was lying face down in the bed with that arm hanging off the side. It ached, and moved beyond the control of his Will, as if blown in a dull, cold wind. Bill Lockridge rolled onto his back. His right arm was wet to the elbow. He sat up and looked around him.

His bed was afloat in a vast, green ocean, frilled white with wavecrests. The moon above glowed emerald and coloured the water around the colour of emerald. The air was sweet with salt and sea-weed.

Gradually, as water lapped over the wooden bedframe, the mattress began to grow heavy with it. The bed began to sink.

The was a snuffling noise, and a splash, from somewhere ahead.

Though the sheets that wrapped her were soaked and cold, Alexus dreamt on. Lockridge touched her shoulder. "Wake up, hon." Somehow he knew that this was her doing.

The splashing grew louder, and he spied the white of troubled waters flowing towards the bed, like a bow-wave around an invisible sailboat.

"Alexus," he said again. "Time to wake up now", and punched her on the arm.

He saw the eyes first, glowing yellow green under the green moon, and then the outlines of the head became clear. The beast was shaped vaguely like an alligator, only three or four times the size. Its head alone was the length of a sofa, covered in a rich ornamentation of wattles, scales, and horns, as though the animal had put on a war helmet.

The eyes swept slowly and impassively over the bed, then stopped at Alexus. Lockridge had the strangest notion that the beast recognised her. It halted, and sniffed at the girl like a big dog, steam curling from its nostrils. Gingerly, the animal bit at the footpost, then lifted its head and dropped the snout onto the bed . Alexus and Lockridge ascended, like they were on one end of a teeter-totter. Bill grabbed at the headboard with one hand and snared the clot of sheets containing Alexus with the other.

"Baby, we're in trouble," he said.

Alexus awoke at this point, though from the content of her own dreams and not, it seemed, at the scene before her. She screamed.

*

"An old boyfriend of yours?" he asked.

"Don't be an asshole," Alexus replied.

Lockridge pulled a tooth about the size of a banana from the wet ruin that had been his bed. "Isn't this something?" he asked, rubbing his finger through the blood on the enamel. "Must be worth a lot. Most of the teeth you see like this are fossilised. How many d'you see that are brand new?"

Alexus had been crying all morning. "Listen," she said finally. "I think we should split up."

"Why?"

She sighed, and rolled her eyes. "Sit down, stupid," she said.

*

She told him about how her life was full of holes, though she didn't usually drink or take drugs. "I don't wear a watch anymore, because constantly resetting the hands makes me sad. I've woken in up so many places, so many different times . . . Once I woke up naked in Central Park in New York City, under a blanket of dead leaves . . . "

"I've woken up in a thousand different beds, besides all sorts of men. I've woken up—and here's where you come in, Bill—where the guy's clothes and his boots and his money and his car keys and his shaving stuff and pictures of me and him in Paris are all over the place, but the guy himself has disappeared. Poof!"

"So I've made my life really simple. I always carry cash in my shoe. I always dress cheap, because I keep losing my wardrobe. I always spend heavy on pleasure, because pleasure is the only thing that's permanent. I always rent; I never buy, because why invest in something you'll only lose? And I know that the quickest way for me to make $10,000 is by taking my clothes off, wherever I am, even in shitholes like St. Pierre . . .

" . . . And I try never to get involved with anyone I like, but I keep screwing that rule up. I need company, I guess."

"Is Alexus your real name?" he asked.

"Oh I don't know. I doubt it."

They sat quietly for a time. "What do we do now?" he asked.

"I leave you," she said, "before I kill you."

He pleaded with her, told her that he would gladly die if it was in her arms. Alexus wept again at his appeals, but finally called for a taxi and left when it arrived.

*

Bill let her go. It all meant nothing because it was a game of hide-and-seek and he knew where Alexus would hide. Thirty minutes later he hopped into his car and drove out to Etobicoke, to the motel strip along its Newmarket border.

The Everett Motel was an L-shaped two-story building that half-surrounded an inner court-yard with a pool at the centre. A chain-link fence covered in vines protected the court-yard from the eyes of the rest of the world. All the local dancers knew of this place. It had a reputation for being safe and accommodating, the rooms Spartan but clean, the staff sympathetic. Alexus had been living here when they had first met, and she was a creature of habit, so he knew that she would return on her first night away from him. Tomorrow, who could say? She was carrying enough money on her to fly around the world eight times in a jet plane.

There was a Sports bar/Strip club called Sneakers across from the Everett. In its sweaty emptiness he found a table overlooking the street, where he could watch the motel entrance through the blinds. At 4:30 p.m. Sneakers was empty. A lonely girl danced on a stage at the back of the place, naked for no purpose, to "Maggie May".

At about 5 p.m. a taxi pulled up to the Everett. Alexus, wearing sun-glasses, a tank-top, and cut-offs, came out of the motel lobby and hopped into it. An hour passed and the cab returned. Alexus exited carrying groceries and, Lockridge noted, a bag from the Liquor Store. That was interesting: Susan had only drank when she was sad. She didn't take to it very well. Half a bottle of wine could knock her out for an evening.

Lockridge hatched a plan. He would wait until Alexus had passed out from the wine, then break into her room and carry her home with him. Since the plan involved waiting, he ordered up some hot wings, and fries, and another drink.

*

"Place closes in an hour. Last call in ten minutes."

Bill's eyes snapped into focus; he looked up at Sable, the waitress, whose bare breasts commingled with the bottles and shooter glasses on her serving tray.

"One more," he said, fumbling through his wallet for a credit card. "Put it all on this."

"You know, honey, there's cheaper ways to get stoned than drinking in a stripper bar and not looking at the strippers."

"It's my fate," he said.

*

The cold night air cleared his head of the smell of cigarettes and puke and furtive masturbation. He walked North, crossed at the light, and picked his way through dim alleyways filled with garbage and busted wooden crates until he had reached the back of the Everett. He climbed the fence and dropped next to one of the lawn chairs around the swimming pool. By day this place would be a vision of heaven, filled with lounging, off-duty strippers.

Lockridge loped quietly towards the building. He told himself that he was meant to be here, meant by Destiny. He wasn't just sneaking around.

Like a shark stroking the surface of the water from underneath, he moved past the identical blue doors that marked the rooms of the Everett and touched them. Inside room 16 "Gun Smoke" was playing on tv. He could hear it faintly when he pressed his ear to the door. That meant channel 3, the oldies. Alexus was inside.

He tapped at the door to room 16 with a single knuckle, holding his breath at the possibilities. If Alexus was awake his plan was blown. She would never let him in; she'd tell him it was for his own good. And if he tried to force the door she would scream.

But there was no response, and he unclenched. The wine had

obviously sent her into a temporary oblivion. And Bill knew his way around locks; he was inside within fifteen seconds.

*

Alexus slept curled up on the bed with her Adidas bag for a pillow. Everything she needed, she had told him, was inside this bag.

The real pillows had been stacked neatly beside the bed. A bottle of cheap white wine, half drank and half spilled, lay on the floor beside them.

Lockridge turned off the television, and fell in beside Alexus. He played with her chest, kissing her through the t-shirt, kissing her on the lips and forehead. But she was out cold. He pulled her t-shirt from her pants and stuck his head underneath. He could have remained like this forever, rocked gently up and down as she breathed.

But his own snoring woke him. The original plan had been to take Melissa home, but he was too drunk for that to happen. So he undressed her, undressed himself, and squeezed her too him until they were like two spoons in a drawer. He bit into her shoulder until she bled but she would not awake. Eventually he surrendered and entered her as she lay unconscious. She was ready, as she always was, warm and deep and wet.

When he was finished the black curtain fell swiftly across his eyes.

*

A series of low, gutty snarls echoed through the ocean from every direction, but Bill was not listening. He was swallowing salt water. He thrashed wildly until he broke surface and could breath again.

Lockridge found himself staring up at an emerald moon, like a jewel pinned to the sky. Tonight, the water was perfectly still and warm as a hot tub. Curls of verdant steam peeled up from its surface.

Fifty yards ahead a gout of white bubbles disturbed the surface, and two yellow eyes appeared in their midst. The ancient gator-thing paddled towards Bill in an leisurely fashion, for there was no shoreline in sight that the man might swim towards.

It eased to a halt about six inches away from him. The two rivals stared at one another.

Lockridge felt a sudden gush of bitterness and betrayal. He choked back a sob.

"She left me," he explained.

# GRAVE DESIRE

## BY DAVID SALCIDO

*"There the wicked cease from troubling; and the weary be at rest."*
—Job iii, 17

They met over dinner, in a most unexpected way. It was on a night when the fog hung heavy and thick over fallow fields, illuminated from without by a misspent Harvest moon. A perfect night for supping and not much more, he had believed. After all, he had arrived late for the feast, hunger gnawing at his belly like a ravenous beast and making him think of nothing else. It is often that way with love.

The banquet still lay spread invitingly, despite his tardiness, and he immediately felt a surge of relief. To the right of the gate, two mangy dogs tussled over a meaty bone and, for a brief moment, he considered entering the fray himself. He was that hungry. But dimly remembered decorum, and the tantalising aromas assailing his nostrils from the still plentiful buffet, kept those urges in check. Bounteous variety lay before him. He had only to pick and choose his drooling heart's desire.

No sooner had he closed in on a particularly mouth-watering morsel, his teeth sweating in anticipation and his mind racing with fevered desire, when he saw her. Like an angel of death she appeared to glow in the half-light, hunkered down over her expertly picked meal, similarly engaged in single-minded and ecstatic repast. Alone, as was the way with their cursed kind, she squatted before her dinner, delicately scooping jellied horror from an exposed eye socket. Her thinning hair lay in disarray and a decaying wedding dress hung in tatters from her thin shoulders. It was at that moment that he knew he had found his one true love.

Stepping lightly over the carnage of the recent battlefield and the brittle cornstalks trampled into mud, blood and excrement, he moved closer, hunger momentarily and uncharacteristically forgotten. Sensing the movement, she looked up and in so doing, locked eyes with her destiny. Her jaw dropped in mid-chew, clear liquid oozing over lips to hang in trembling dollops from a charmingly skeletal chin. As if in a dream state, he unconsciously brought his hands up to straighten what was left of the dusty and stained bow tie to his shredded tuxedo. Perfect. She was perfect, in so many ways.

Stepping forward, he lowered himself into a squat before her, his gummy yellow eyes never leaving hers. In response, she lifted, with a gore-slick right hand, a mass of muscle and congealing plasma, and laid it gently into his waiting hands. He broke the mesmerising gaze he held with her to look down at the gift. A heart. Still whole and unsullied. A token of her affection and, perhaps, more. Smiling, he lifted the favour to his mouth and wasted no time in devouring it greedily.

Satisfied, she lowered her head to bite the lips off the corpse before her, then sat back to watch him as she chewed. And so it went, throughout most of the night, the two of them sharing their finds, wordless and united in a preordained ritual of despair and desecration. The wedding feast of eyes, teeth and rapidly swelling bellies gave rise to a bond promising more, much more to come. In the distance, a dog howled, joined by another, then another. Overcome by emotion, even as his nature drove him to perform the ultimate sacrilege, he bowed his head in thanks for the hopeful redemption he had found.


And finally, when the meal was done, and their unsavoury hungers abated, she cocked her head to the side. Wisps of frazzled blonde hair waved fetchingly from a head gone almost completely bald, as she reached up with trembling fingers to push the wedding dress from her emaciated shoulders. As it slipped unhindered to the ground with a rustle of finality, she stood exposed before him in the glow of the fog-enshrouded moon, and lowered her head demurely.

She was, to his caked and putrid eyes, the most beautiful thing he had ever seen. Her withered breasts hung flat and empty upon her ribcage. Her distended stomach bulged obscenely beneath them, filled to capacity and beyond. Her legs, free of sinew or girlish curve, tacked as they were below hollow, hatchet-like hips, appeared incapable of supporting such weight. And yet, to him, she was a long-awaited goddess.

Fumbling with the rope, which held his pants in place, he soon stood in a puddle of rotted cloth, his withered member jutting out before him expectantly. She raised her head and nodded at the offering. Stepping forward, she helped him rid himself of the tuxedo coat and shirt. The bow tie she left in place, drooping in dejected formality across pronounced collarbone. Soon he was as naked as she and, after a chaste kiss was attempted between thin, dry, formless lips, she began to pull him down to the charred and blood-soaked ground. He followed willingly, and in so doing, sealed his fate.

Running her hands over her willing supplicant with a sound like leaves skittering across gravestones, she lowered her face to his nether regions. Inhaling deeply of the musty decay and filth, which arose to assault her senses, she began first kissing and licking at the wasted genitals with a surprisingly agile tongue. Then as the passion of the moment overtook her, she began nipping and biting, making him squirm with anticipation. Her ministrations became frenzied and soon she was rooting feverishly into his groin, a vibration like the rattling of bones rising up to merge with his unearthly moans, until finally the shrivelled penis came loose.

He screamed through the ecstasy, never looking away from the bright glowing orb swimming in the milky and oppressively close sky. Gripping her scaly head tightly, he pressed her face deeper between his legs, yellowed eyes gleaming with long-forgotten tears. Emboldened by his gratification, she made short work of his deteriorated testicles and fervently attacked the swollen bladder which was his stomach. Working her way upward toward the birthplace of his sin, she revelled in the ecstasy of their union by devouring every organ offered her one by one.

As the music of their lovemaking filled the night, frightening children and committing mothers to their rosaries, he howled an orgasmic thank you to the gods of darkness for granting him this unexpected reprieve from deathless wandering. And, as has always been the case where true love is concerned, his curse became his saving grace.

# IS THERE LIFE ON MARS?

## BY M.F. KORN & HERTZAN CHIMERA

Once the astronaut planted his boot on the surface of Mars he glee-fully smiled as faecal silage dripped into the reservoir in the back of his suit. He knew he was helmet-miked up to the whole planet Earth, but unfortunately all he managed to say was "I'm shitting in my pants, Jezus, that freeze-dried shit . . . " The rehearsed line was supposed to be "Man has conquered the stars . . . "

He could hear them giggling, all his old school chums, all the guys at the local dairy cream, his priest, his fugging mother in law with her horsey holler; four guys back at mission control spat out their cof-fees and this fused the connection to his helmet-mike, leaving him chilled by the sudden silence.

He looked about him, "You know, what it boils down to is . . . shit happens." He didn't realise it was Mars->Earth connection that was shot like a dead dog, he was still transmitting live to radio receivers all over Earth and he would only know the truth upon his triumphant and unbelievable return home.

He saw Crippin in the module-pod busting a gut laughing. The radio came back online: " . . . Don't worry, old sport, there is prob-ably delay enough that Mission Control covered your brilliant line up . . . "

"I hope so. I've got to come back in there and change, there is dribbling vile spittle inside my legsters . . . "

"Okay."

The linkup ship shot by overhead and disappeared over the FDR mountain range.

"Hey, we are close enough to see that FACE on MARS rock, aren't we?"

"Yeah, it's right over there. But you know what the bosses at Mission Control said; it's total bullshit and there's no time for silliness. Come on in, old sport."

The module-pod's brass iris opened underneath the leg-sheaths, where Youngblood could grapple up the ladder and recompress. He got inside and undressed, vacuuming the shit off his ass with the special sucking gadget both men and women use out here in the toss end of space. Man has conquered the stars—it was something he had been conscientiously rehearsing for months. He tried to say it again,

"Man has conquered the stars." He Royal-Shakespeared, loud and proud, right hand to his chest, left hand aloft. In walked Crippin a washing peg on his nose like an idiot.

"Christ, Cripp, don't you ever ease up on a bloke?" Youngblood whined, his limp cock still had a bit of minestrone bottom-soup dangling from it that Crippin made a gesture towards with his eyes. Idiot Youngblood couldn't believe how shit the day had gone. This was his chance to shine and all he could do was drop a load in his gold inlaid surface gear.

All at once the module-pod lifted off, making both Crippin and Youngblood stagger to one side of the ship.

"Christ, Cripp, that dumn bitch is gonna whiplash the lot of us one of these days."

"I heard that, you turnkey sellers." Hanoi Jane rang out on the tannoy. She hauled the pod-module out over toward tranquillity plain where the mountainous shadowlands known on Earth as the face on mars hung about in uneasy slumber. It was minus 205 degrees in the shade.

"Jane, did you get permish from Bossman central to suddenly take off like that?" grated Youngblood into his collar-stick.

"You little buggers, I knew you shit in your pants and climbed back in . . . I wasn't gonna leave ya."

"That fugging man-woman! You gotta go by the rules!" Youngblood offloaded to Crippen. They managed to hold on as the module levelled out and skittered over the surface steady at 500 meters altitude.

"Youngie, you know how she feels about seeing that Elvis face or rockface or whatever. Bossman control is screaming at us right now. I hear em comin' in on another band! It's that asshole Ben Dodge, P.R. guy sayin' we were unprofessional."

"Screw that fat fuck! I couldn't help it. That creamed chipped beef went through me like shit through a goose!"

They heard Hanoi Jane yelling through their collar-sticks: "Whooohooo! Weeeheee! Elvise come ta mama!"

They sailed over the crest of a ridge of hills into the valley of the shadowlands where the Face on Mars was waiting for them like a hyena; cunning, relentless. The Sun exploded over the ridge in a huge blast of ultra violet. At least they thought it was the Sun. Youngblood had just fitted himself back into a pressurised shell suit and Crippin was beside him, scratching his balls far too slowly, like he was trying to drain the juice from his scrotal sack. Like time had slowed to a crawl. Crippin looked worried then. A frown creased his forehead and continued to crease his forehead more and more until he was screaming as his head imploded.

"What's the fuggin static?!?!?" Hanoi Jane was shrieking at the top of her voice. Swiftly, her tannoy voice was lopped off, decapitated. Youngblood watched as the craggy surface of the Face of Mars swept up to meet his broken module-pod. When he should have panicked and filled his shell suit, all he could pass was gas. But even the gas was contaminated by fate's unreal atmosphere. It had a passionate allure that made him forget that he was plummeting to his death. Crippin wasn't yet dead and he made one last gesture to communicate with base, his hand on his collar-stick trembled as he croaked an unintelligible garble down the frequency.

The module-pod hit the Martian surface in complete silence.

Youngblood found himself in a mercury pool of confusion. The air worked all wrong, worrying his lungs. There was a vague sense of imbalance and he knew if he moved he would surely vomit again. Wherever he was, it smelled of the most beautifully sweat vomit he had ever known. Brownian motion the flavour of vanilla pod filled his vision and he heard music but not music, not arrhythmic twangs but caramel melodies filled with swirling emotions abstracted by need. He had no idea which way was up or what had happened.

There lay Crippin in a nutter butter Elvis banana sandwich of blood.

Hanoi Jane he saw was floating above the ship, and by God on Toast she was wiggling her pelvis with a sort of bodice or corporeal but ephemeral ghostlike apparition in a white sequinned jumpsuit, dyed black hair though transparent, and Youngblood heard blasts of "Hound Dog", "Ain't nuthin' but a Hound Dog, Crying all the time". All manner of realtime coordinates of existence were nil, it was all a surreal pastiche either in his broken helmet and bleeding forehead, or he was dead already. But there was Hanoi Jane, and she wasn't even wearing her suit, because she never suited up during this unreal impromptu flight and crash.

The rock face was beneath his feet; he believed he was sitting atop as the module-pod had crashed. How did he get out of the ship? How could he be alive and not guacamole boiled alive and flash frozen if his helmet plate was cracked and open to the harshness? The rockface hummed like a tesla generator from God. That is what he imagined. And all he could do was look at dead Crippin and Hanoi Jane a-rockin' and a-jukboxin' with some Elvis phantom of unreality that resembled himself. He even had the birth mark on his back, the silhouette of a fruit bat choking on a fig or something similar, all Rorschach and mind bait.

Flip flop went reality and dream emulsifying into some sort of body porridge. One minute he was dying in the wreckage of the module-pod, the next he was floating off into the ether hand in hand with Hanoi Jane the singer of the King's songs, the hummer of birds. They appeared to swoop up a great slope, cherubs following on after them like turbulence in the parallel universe they were clearly skimming. They rubbed up again the gossamer membrane separating this material world and that ephemeral plane and little sonnets of tune and dramas of light and shade leapt off the walls constricting tighter and tighter in. Hanoi Jane turned a bright smiling face on our hero. Her smile disintegrated in a leaf falling extravaganza of boiling sunlight reflecting in the cornea of an infant. The filaments drifted away and a deafening static hiss burst into his head like ringworm, decaying his mental faculties so that he couldn't even analyse the photonic stream to make sense of his dreamy waking state.

He reached out for Hanoi Jane but she was not there. In her place something shifted, like a winter stoat beneath a sheath of russet leaves, a mole disturbing topsoil, veinfillers inflating under the flesh, eyepoppers filling the cranial cavities infusing his skull porridge with another ugly shade of cultural gloom.

They opened their mouths to utter welcome all at once and he thought his puny head would not take the strain such was the decibellic anti-gravity. Every neurone inside his memory of mankind shook, rattled and rumbled threatening rupture. Molecules of cerebral transmission fled the area like rats leaving a sinking ship. Surely he was dying. Is dead. Should be reborn as a cat. Will never claw his way out of his makeshift grave. They exploded every single atom in his body when they lifted his head into their warm embrace—he thought he had an Elvis hair lip in this extradimension, parodying the wild man of rock pelvising. He tripped out on the one tune singularity in the back of his humanity called nostalgia. One spark dwindling to a single dot of Buckminsterfullerine, no internal substance just a microfine black shell.

Welcome to my world . . . he heard the Elvis mania rushing through his fabric . . . won't you come on in? miracle of sin, should happen now and then . . . Wasn't that Jim Reeves? He swung this way and that in his disorientation . . . Could they be using his memory of music as a means to communication? What was the syntax? How could he find a picture postcard to reply to? What ink would his monologue colour taste like? Battery acid for the tongue of rhythm and rhyme, he felt his edge being tipped over . . .

As Youngblood breathed in vacuum now, his powdered bodice twitched its last. A thousand miles across, with the pod module on top of the huge edifice of the face, the entire rock face creaked and smiled a handsome Elvis Presley smile along igneous rock fissures in the topographic blemishes of the fulgurite pitted river beds, in the blasted heath of Mars.

# THE FACE IN THE CROWD

## BY DEAN R. HEWISH

Hi, I'm Jack, pleased to meet you. Well, that's not really my name. In my line of business, we know that names are like spit, bits of hair and fingernail clippings; someone can use them to make a voodoo doll. Get power over you. Of course, it's all done electronically nowadays.

I know that's a strange thing to say. You see; I'm in Intelligence. I'm a spy, a spook, a secret agent. Really.

I work for an Agency you have never heard of, but we get our orders from an Agency that you have definitely heard of. Unless you kept your head in the sand for the past twenty years or so.

What do I actually do? It's not what you think. We don't scuttle around in trench coats and black hats messing with coded messages; dead letter drops, photographing top-secret documents and that stuff. That's only on TV. We just do research. We scan the newspapers, the electronic media, sometimes mobile phone conversations. Oh yes, we look at Web pages and e-mail too. We look for anything that might be a threat to the security of this great nation of ours. I'm being serious. I really believe that we're helping to preserve the best damn country in the world.

Is it okay for me to be telling you this? No worries. Everybody knows we're doing those kinds of things. It's been in all the papers.

Ah, you use encryption on your private e-mail so nobody can eavesdrop.

Sorry, a bit of my drink must have gone down the wrong way. What were we talking about? Yes, encryption. Sure, makes your stuff secure. Keep it up.

I'm all right, it happened again. No, I wasn't laughing. Honest.

I'll tell you, I love my job. I know it's out of fashion to feel that way these days but that's how it is. I got recruited while I was still at university, doing an arts degree. I never found out why they picked me. It couldn't have been my marks. Someone must have noticed me in the debating society or the political club. Anyway, they told me that they would pay all my fees and give me a bit extra as a living allowance. Plus a steady job once I finished if I shaped up. What do you think I said? Do I look stupid? An offer like that is better than gold these days. The only down side was that I had to go away for tests and training a couple of weeks every year. I must have passed the tests, because it all went as they said it would.

So, I started work. It's an office like any other. The other people are easy to get on with and we're given a fair bit of freedom to go poking around at things that catch our interest. Sometimes really important stuff comes out of that.

The only thing that bothered me at first was that every now and then one of the newer people like me would have what we called the Psycho Month. Sometimes you could see it coming. Suddenly the person would get this sort of worried, haunted look. He or she would go to the Controller. The Controller would have all of their current projects reassigned, then the person would spend a month or a bit less in their office with the door closed, not talking and staying glued to the computer screen, scrolling through masses of data. We even had an icon to go with it. They would stick this picture of Alfred E. Neuman from Mad Magazine on the door to warn people to stay away. At the end of the month, the person would go to the Controller and have a long talk, then go back to work as though nothing had happened. Nobody would tell us newbies what it was all about. Ask the people who had gone through it what the big secret was and they would smile beatifically and clam up. One funny thing I noticed was that a couple of them seemed to get agitated when we went out for drinks after work. Acted as though they felt uncomfortable in crowds. Kept looking around when they thought you weren't watching them.

We new people would joke about it but we just didn't have a clue and guessed that it was some kind of breakdown, information overload or something. It scared us a bit. Anyway, I thought that I was too smart and on the ball to have it happen to me. It turned out that being on the ball was just the problem.

I was working on this operation. We were targeting a big drug cartel boss. I'll call him Carlos; aren't they all. Nothing like his real name, but neither were the names on his credit cards and passports. We had inside information that he was about to come here to personally set up this end of a mega-size smuggling operation. Trouble was, nobody had been able to pin him down at a place and a time.

That was my job.

I was going through pictures collected by surveillance cameras. You wouldn't believe how much coverage there is, these days. Airports, train stations, shopping plazas, streets; everywhere. Of course, all the tapes, disks and files from the cameras are shared through joint arrangements with other Agencies all over.

Nobody notices the cameras, just like they don't really notice the people around them. Crowded places like airports are empty spots in our lives. Everybody walks around with blank expressions on their faces and never looks anybody else in the eye. It works in our favour. Sometimes we manage to catch the scumbags off guard in places like that.

Most of the time, the computer did my work for me. We had a picture of someone that we were sure was Carlos and the computer had made this three-dimensional model of his head. It was rotating in the bottom corner of the screen. Then I had it flick through the camera pictures real fast and the artificial intelligence software tried to match the heads with the model. It was pretty good at it too, even with shots taken from the back.

Sure, computers aren't that smart yet. Your computers aren't that smart. Wait a year or two, or six months. Whatever.

While the computer was doing its job, I had to keep reviewing the pictures myself. The computer was real good, but sometimes it missed things that a person can pick up easy as anything. Our brains are wired to recognise faces.

The machine and I were doing a top-notch job. We had Carlos nailed in a mass of airport pictures and I was constructing a really detailed map of his movements. I got it almost up to date so I knew exactly where he was. It looked as though we had a good chance of predicting exactly where and when he was going to arrive. I had already sent the summary off to our people in Strategic Planning.

Then I noticed something. In one of the pictures of Carlos, he was standing next to somebody who looked familiar. It was a man, looking like any other face in the crowd. His face sort of rang a bell, but I really couldn't match a name to it. Just somebody I thought I had seen before. I started scanning through other pictures where Carlos was present. Sure enough, the stranger turned up in one of those. I had the computer grab his likeness and do an automated search. The guy was in a surprising number of places. Okay, I thought, this must be some associate of Carlos we had never picked up on before. Or maybe some overseas Agency had beaten us to the punch and already had one of their men tailing Carlos. That could be a big help, except it would have been nicer if they had warned us they were running an op. Just to be sure, I checked through our files of known good guys and bad guys. Nobody matched.

I had to take the results of the job I did on Carlos to the Controller, so I printed out a blow up of the face of the mystery man and took it along with me. I showed it to him and asked if he knew anything that would help me work out who the guy was.

His reaction would have been funny if it hadn't scared the shit out of me. He put his head down on his arm on the desk and thumped the desk with his other fist. Then he sat up. He had this sort of funny lop-sided grin on his face.

"Okay," he said. "Should have known you would get to it on this operation. Listen, here's how it works. You have thirty days. Maybe you'll come up with something new this time."

I thought, Christ, the Psycho Month. What's going on?

He opened his desk drawer and handed me the Alfred E. Neuman icon.

"I'll reassign all your projects. You can do whatever you like. Go hot air ballooning if you think that's what it takes, but when you are ready or in thirty days max, you come to me and we talk it over. Then you get back to work and forget all about it. Do you agree?"

Of course, I said yes, but I was shaking in my shoes and had no idea what he was talking about.

He slid the picture of the mystery man back across the desk to me and I picked it up. Obviously, I was being dismissed, so I walked out with the picture and the silly icon.

I had to go through with the charade. I put the icon up on my door and shut myself in. I sat down and stared into space, then I stared at the picture. It all had something to do with the mystery man. Right, that was the starting point. I already had the computer primed, so I updated the profile using the other shots of the guy I'd turned up and managed to get a half decent 3D reconstruction, just like the one of Carlos that I had been using. Then I set the computer to work trying to track the bastard to find out where he came from. This kind of work takes time. There are literally billions of individual frames to sift through. Next day I got the second shock of the week. Normally we reckon we're getting real lucky if we come up with three or four pictures of the target. I had done much better with Carlos, but we already knew he was on the move and had a fair idea of where to start. But this guy turned up like everywhere.

I left the computer going at it while I tried to come to grips with the task over the next week. Standard practice was to create a chart of movements. Dates, times, places. Some bits were easy. Most cameras put a date and time stamp on the picture. Others from low rent localities didn't, and then I had to call up the file and check its date. Otherwise, there might be a date on the tape or disk that was filed in Archives. It was usually the date and time it was finished, so I would have to start at the end and count the days backward, using lighting or people density as clues. You get good at it really quickly.

When you have a chart, you can match ground transport time-tables or flight numbers and really get inside the target's head. I could see right away that it just wasn't going to work. There had to be more than one of them. I worked on the chart but it quickly began looking like a network, not a path, so I put it aside. I had evidence that at least two of them were in a few of the places at the same time. By now, I was starting to understand the funny look that people had on their faces during Psycho Month. I knew that I was getting it myself.

The face kept bothering me. As I said, I sort of recognised it but couldn't remember where I had seen it. Early middle age, no obvious racial or ethnic group, kind of handsome, short dark hair, a bit tanned. I needed the best photograph that I could get. Ah: Singapore's Changi Airport. State of the art camera system, lovely definition, brilliant colour. I found a picture of one of the guys. A great full face shot. I increased the mag, then had the computer run a clean up on the image. I looked closely at it and the feeling of familiarity came again.

I suppose that's what put me on to it. I don't known how it occurred to me to do the trick, but I started grabbing faces at random off the files. Then I had the computer superimpose them and add them up. Pretty quickly, it became obvious that I had hit on the solution. The more faces I added, the closer the picture came to looking like my man. I started mixing in more racial types and that helped even more. These guys were a statistical average of the human male population. No wonder I had that feeling of familiarity. They had something of everybody I had ever seen.

Shit, I thought, is a plastic surgeon running a business giving people average faces as some sort of ultimate disguise? What if these people are human clones or something? I knew that something weird was going on, but I needed more information.

By this time, I was regularly working late and realised that I was acting absolutely true to type for the person in the office with the Psycho icon.

I had to get back to tracing the people to find out what they were doing, now that I knew the rules of the game. I could find them in airports, railway stations and public squares. Not in food malls, or at least not at the serving counters, but that didn't bother me. Maybe they didn't like fast food. I decided to concentrate on the airports. Not only do airports have great camera coverage, but also it's easier to match locations with flights and destinations because airline bookings are all computerised. Then we can cross-correlate passenger lists and get to the magic names. I picked up one of the guys and ran backward and forward in time to try to see where he came from and went. It just got weirder. Sure, I could more or less track him in and around the terminal, but he never turned up at a departure gate or check-in counter. Never caught him getting in or out of ground transport. Other places drew a blank as well, like eating places and toilets.

There are no cameras in toilets? Think again. Modern cameras can be smaller than a button on your shirt. You never see them. Just remember to smile, okay?

I ran this procedure on a few others in different airports and always found the same thing. It started to scare me. What sort of person hangs around in an airport terminal but never gets on a plane.

Yeah, airport staff. But even they have to leave or go to the bathroom sometime. Anyway, they're easy to pick. They are always trying to look important.

Right, it was time to get complete pictures of some of them. Up until now, I had concentrated on the faces but perhaps there were clues in what they were wearing or carrying. Singapore came to the rescue again. I found a whole body shot of one and enhanced it. Average build, naturally. Dark business suit, plain dark tie, shiny black shoes. No hand luggage. A rather elaborate watch on the left wrist and a camera hanging around the neck. It was hard to find another top quality full body picture, but it seemed that they were all dressed alike and carried similar watches and cameras.

What sort of camera was it? I wondered. That Singapore picture looked like the best I was going to get so I digitally cut the camera out of the picture and ran some heavy-duty image enhancement on it. You remember when NASA fucked up big time and sent the space telescope into orbit with bad optics? Red faces all round, but they tried to compensate by whipping their programmers into working out some truly magic image enhancement procedures. Of course, I had all those and better on my machine. It's called deconvolution and we used to joke that we could pull the Mona Lisa out of a Jackson Pollock.

I got a great picture of the camera but it was moderately uninformative. The camera had no identifying logo and looked much like lots of cameras you see in store windows. That's right, it looked like any camera but it wasn't a camera you could go out and buy. Believe me, I tried. I hawked the picture around dozens of camera stores. They tried to sell me almost everything they had on the shelves, but they could never give me what I asked for. There are none on the market that matched it exactly, nor have there ever been. It was harder to get a good look at the watch but I suspected that it went the same way.

There, the guys were an average and the cameras were generic. That's if the things were really cameras at all.

I had an idea. I called up female faces and averaged them then had the computer do a search. I knew even before it started what would happen. Sure enough, there were female versions wandering around. Similar places, similar movement patterns. Roughly the same numbers. Not in the bars or toilets.

I know; peeking in women's toilets is sick. Had to be done, though. I don't like it either. I got the computer to handle that automatically.

The females were attractive, same general age as the men, dressed in dark business clothes as well. Medium length skirt, same camera, perhaps a slightly smaller watch. Like the men, they all had neutral expressions on their faces. They didn't smile, frown, or give any other sign of emotion. But then, the people around them had much the same expressions. And that was the point. They were never alone. You always found them in groups of people.

So far as I could tell, the men and the women didn't get together. In fact, none of them ever got together. I can't recall seeing even a single frame that took in two of them. They didn't seem to talk to anybody at all.

That's about when I hit the brick wall. I knew these people existed but nothing much else about them made sense. All my probing had achieved was to bring up a list of things they didn't do. I truly couldn't find any way forward and my month was nearly up, so I collected my notes and print outs and knocked on the Controller's door.

He looked relieved.

"Well, that's about average," he said. "Let's look at what you got."

I showed him the pictures and my charts.

He looked pleased. "You're sharp. Not everybody works out the averaging trick, so sometimes they don't pick up that there are both males and females," he said.

I told him about the movement patterns. How I couldn't work out how they travelled around and how they were missing from the very places you would most expect to find them.

"Who are these people?" I asked.

"Perhaps 'what are these things' might be a better way to phrase the question," he replied.

I had to pick my jaw up off the floor. I genuinely hadn't thought of that.

"So what do we know about them?" I asked when I got my voice back.

"Not much more than you've shown me today," he said. "This is the way it is," he continued. "Ever since intelligence organisations have been scanning security photographs, operatives have been turning these mannequins up. All the Agencies started schemes like

Psycho Month so that their people could get it out of their system once and for all. If we just alerted every new operative when they arrived, they'd probably keep looking for the things and it would distract them from their real tasks. You're totally sick and tired of them now and never want to see their dopey faces again, correct?"

"Yeah, that the truth," I replied.

"We also use it as a kind of proficiency test," he said, smiling at me. "Congratulations, you passed."

I didn't feel inclined to smile back.

"Look, why don't we just pull one or two of these people or things in for questioning?" I asked.

He laughed. "It's been tried. We made ourselves real unpopular with the other Agency when we asked them to grab a few. They would pick out the guy or woman and close in but, when they got there, the target had evaporated. Nobody ever saw it happen, but they were always in a crowd and the things just seemed to merge with a group of people and never came out the other side. They tried being subtle, putting tails on them. Same thing happened. It didn't matter how many of their people they used in the operation. The agents accused us of running some fool conjuring trick to make them look stupid."

I felt cold all over. "Shit, that's creepy," I said. "Where do they come from? What do we think they're doing here?"

"We've run all sorts of scenarios, but who knows. They might just be tourists. They could be spies checking us out before the big whammy, God forbid. Maybe they're anthropologists. Heck, perhaps they're ghosts who stick around for the company. Take your pick. So far, we don't think they are doing any harm. We don't seem to be able to touch them and the Agency's policy is to ignore them. And that's what I want you to do from now on, is that clear?" he finished, glaring at me.

"Yes boss," I replied and handed him back the Psycho icon.

Well, that was the end of the affair, so far as my work was concerned. I knew better than to pursue the matter any further and the other stuff I was doing was far more important. At least in the opinion of the Agency, and that's all that counts in my world.

But I couldn't let it go completely. I took to hanging around the airport lounge in my spare time, acting just like the mystery things. It made me wonder, were these things intelligence operatives who had seen something strange in a security scan and started haunting public places, eventually sort of blending into the world average. No, that wasn't right. I still had to eat and go to the toilet.

It took a while, but then I turned around and there he was. There was absolutely no doubt. We were in a fairly thick crowd, but I had a clear path and started toward him. He saw me and knew I was on to him. I could see it in his face, though his expression didn't change. He looked me straight in the eye. He didn't hurry; he just turned and moved off into the mass of people. I was hot on his heels when this big guy got in the way. I shouldered him aside but he protested and grabbed my arm. I yelled "Security" at him, yanked the ID badge out from inside my shirt and shoved it in his face. I swear that I had at least part of the mystery thing in sight at all times, but when the big guy let me go and I rushed on, there was not a trace.

Oh, well. It wasn't as if I hadn't been warned. I had to try it out for myself, though.

Then I came here.

None of this is true, of course. This is just another bullshit story dreamed up by a drunk in a bar to pass the time while he gets plastered. I don't care whether you believe me or not. The Agency apparently doesn't care either. But think about this for a minute. Remember what I said about names? Well, I've told you that there are things walking around out there among us and we can't find out their names. Only, I'd sleep better at night if I could be certain that they don't know ours.

Another drink? Thanks. Make it a double scotch like the last. And the one before that.

# 300,000 MOMENTS OF PAIN

## BY JEFFREY THOMAS

Eastborough, Massachusetts has a population of 15,649. That breaks down to about 743 people per square mile. And when at work we produce a batch of the dental anaesthesia Eastocaine, typically consisting of 300,000 syringe cartridges, that works out to be about 20 painful shots of pain killer per citizen. A hurtful bit of numbness, like the burn of heroin in a vein, cocaine in a nose, whiskey in a throat.

Not to say, of course, that the magical solutions we produce are used in our town alone. EastCoast Pharmaceuticals is the fourth largest pharmaceutical company in the United States. In employee meetings, profits are referred to in the matter of billions. I remember being a new employee and marvelling at talk, during these meetings, that the company owned this or that molecule. (One images a microscopic flag planted on such a molecule. Though I suppose I own my own molecules.) I was even more in awe of the building, seeing it up close for the first time, though as a resident of Eastborough I had driven by it on countless occasions. The sprawling complex of buildings—either utterly windowless or else made entirely of windows—is dominated by an immense glass pyramid, a striking sight, looming against the sky behind it and mirroring that sky whether it be brilliantly blue or midnight black. On days when thick fog comes in off nearby Lake Pometacomet, the pyramid is only a vague but still towering mystery against its paler grey background, like an ethereal echo of itself.

As a lifelong townie, I could tell you a lot about the reputation

Eastborough has for weirdness. Maybe it's something in the water, or the magnetic ley lines in the earth itself. There are certain spots, certain places, that seem to have generated more tales of hauntings and murder and unexplained events than others. The print shop Rosen Thermographers, where I also worked for a time, comes quickly to mind . . . though the scariest thing I personally encountered there were the wages and the management. There was that employee who came to work with a gun, for instance (fortunately, before my stint), and the mysterious fire that ultimately gutted the place. Another seemingly psychically polluted spot would of course be Eastborough Swamp. Less known as such a place, unless you work there yourself, is EastCoast Pharmaceuticals.

*

EastCoast is a melting pot. I recall the very rewarding feeling I had one night, riding to a local doughnut shop during our 1:15 AM third shift "lunch", sitting in the back seat with my Laotian group leader Patty, while Fazal, an Indian Muslim, and Ufuk, a Turkish Muslim, sat up front . . . Fazal and Patty singing, "Ooh baby I love your way", along with Peter Frampton on the radio. If only we could all ride along together in such harmony on this fast-spinning globe of ours as it hurtles us to that great doughnut shop in the sky! Most of my co-workers are from Ghana, and seem to me a bit moody at times but are generally very polite, very articulate, very nice to work with; in my immediate team there are Ama, Daniel, and Frederick. But last year the new guy in our department, Chris, was just a boring old native-born Anglo-Saxon white boy like me. Well, we were immigrants, too . . . we'd simply got here several generations before the likes of Ufuk and Ama.

I trained Chris on the cartridge washer in Bay Three, and we hit it off right away, both being avid readers who would generally prefer to crack a book on our break time than hobnob with our co-workers, however pleasant they were. Like me, Chris tended to get philosophical about the thousands upon thousands of injectable 1.8 ml cartridges we produced of such patented solutions as Eastocaine Hydrochloride in water. Chris and I were struck by the irony of the night Ama was suffering intensely from an impacted wisdom tooth, at the same time being surrounded by countless gallons of medicine which might have relieved her agony.

Our job was to operate the washer, which sanitised the empty glass disposable cartridges and lubricated them with silicone before sending them through the wall into the sterile core to be filled. When they re-emerged, we would load the filled product into trays and onto wagons. Like me, Chris marvelled at the dumpsters in Bay One, filled with defective and rejected fully constructed syringes (imposingly large) of morphine sulphate (a junkie's vision of heaven; I could imagine one of them diving head first into such a dumpster to die in unparalleled bliss). All those needles that would never pierce flesh. All the many more that would. All the pain they would bring before the comfort that followed. People fear needles. We manufacture fear here at EastCoast Pharmaceuticals, as if mass-producing sacrificial knives inside a great Aztec ziggurat.

Chris was a divorcee, and didn't seem to want to get into the subject much further than that fact, but we would trade sexually-themed jokes at times, as males will do to bond. When we were caught up on our work and sat in the SOP room reading from the numerous volumes of Standard Operating Procedures (crenated impressions across our foreheads, left by our hair coverings, looking like scars where the top of our skulls had been sawed off and our brains removed—or so it felt, working on third shift), we would joke about the lists of terms that defined defective products. I'd read the term, and Chris would supply his suggestive interpretation. There was "poor self support structure" ("Better use Viagra!" Chris would quip), "non/ slow function" ("More Viagra!"), "crooked plunger" ("Ouch!"), "no orifice" ("Bummer!"), "finger grip slippage" ("Hold onto that thing!"), "needle sheath can not be removed" ("My condom's caught in my pubic hair!"), "protruding plunger" ("Down, boy!"), "plunger motion exceeds limits" ("She's had enough, already!"), "sloppy fill" ("No comment!"), "soiled unit" ("Sorry, wrong hole . . . "), "discoloured needle sheath" (" . . . but at least I used a rubber!"), "scuffed/ scratched tube" ("Watch those teeth!"), "loose plunger rod" ("You promiscuous stud, you!"), "poor rod formation", "channel leaker", "blocked orifice", "invaginated stopper" (?!) and so on.

We are haunted by ourselves. There was something haunted—distantly morose—in Chris that I couldn't pick up on, though it may have had to do with his ex wife, or his general sensitivity. He seemed to have a half-formed crush on a pretty East Indian woman who sat at another table during break, and maybe on an Asian named Lee, too (but then every guy, myself included, liked long-haired Lee). Chris admitted he found foreign-born women exotic. But he never approached any of these co-workers, that I was aware of.

When one night during lunch one of the solution preps joined us at our table and mentioned that she'd received some more mysterious phone calls upstairs last Friday night, Chris's interest was really piqued. He asked us what that was in reference to, and the rest of us were only too quick to launch into the stories of EastCoast's alleged hauntings. Most of these tales were related by Ama in her dark and musical Ghanian accent (with a touch of British from the four years she'd lived in London).

Ama explained how on Friday nights, when third shift was a mere skeleton crew, there were occasionally phone calls to solution prep which, when answered, resulted in only empty silence.

Someone playing tricks? Chris suggested. But Ufuk jumped in to relate how a security guard had once been making his rounds, crossing from the guard shack to the main complex, when he saw the glass elevator rising through the glass pyramid. As he drew closer, he saw it descend again. But when he entered the pyramid to investigate, he found no one in any of its offices.

The solution prep who had brought up the phone calls added that they often heard noises on the floor above them on Friday nights when there should be no one on that level.

Ama jumped back in to say that she once saw a computer in a darkened office go on by itself, as she was passing along a corridor lined with such offices, deserted for the night.

Someone recounted how one evening, three second shift co-workers decided to take a walk in the woods in back of the company, where they bordered on Lake Pometacomet. A voice in the woods shouted at them, as if to purposely ward them off, and they went running back to their building in fright.

Supposedly, Ufuk said, EastCoast was built on a Native American burial ground. Chris groaned, but I told him that as a kid I had always heard legends that Lake Pometacomet—named after Chief Sachem Pometacomet, also known as "King Phillip", who declared war on the white man's colonies—was haunted. Allegedly, a young Indian woman had once drowned or killed herself or been murdered in that lake, falling or jumping or being pushed from a canoe in its very centre. What wasn't a rumour was that EastCoast used to dump its waste water into Lake Pometacomet, until it was told to stop and had to pay for the lake's restoration.

Chris grew increasingly intrigued, and rather less sceptical, at the sheer volume of stories so many of us had to add. Still, he asked reasonably, why would a ghost or ghosts haunt inside so modern, so high tech a place as EastCoast? Well, I said, one time on the way to the town dump I saw a coyote run across the road, and because I live a few streets over from the aforementioned Eastborough Swamp, some nights I've heard coyotes howling in the woods. This town, this whole country, is over-developed. There just aren't enough old Victorian houses and 18th century graveyards left to contain all the ghosts anymore. The spirits have been driven into more developed areas, like the coyotes with their shrinking habitats.

Chris laughed uneasily at my theory (even though I had Ufuk nodding thoughtfully), and he faced Ama as she returned to the subject of the security guard who had seen the elevator operating by itself, as if a ghost were playing with a device that was alien to it, like the phones and computers.

One time, she told him, the security guard had again been making his rounds when he heard a woman sobbing inside a locked storage closet.

The guard hadn't tried unlocking the closet. And he had quit, Ama said, shortly thereafter.

*

One night Chris showed me an article he had torn out of a newspaper left on a table in our gigantic cafeteria (did I mention it has a triangular-shaped fountain pool in its centre?) The article concerned recent findings about the water strider insect, and seemed to illustrate some point Chris was trying to make about the relationships between men and women. It didn't seem to make sense, biologically, he said, for men to be more obsessed with sex than women were. Wasn't it all about procreation, propagating the species? But the water strider story seemed to help him understand this conflict. It seems that male water striders had been evolving a more flattened abdomen and longer, gripping genitalia to make them more adapted for overpowering females for mating. However, in an evolutionary process that countered that other process, as if two Gods were at war over the same species, females had been adapting new features that made it increasingly difficult for the males to mate with them. It seemed contradictory, but it was all worked out, no doubt, to maintain a balance in numbers, in population, in Nature as a whole. So Chris said.

Um, your point being? I asked him. He sort of shrugged it off beyond that information, however. All he really added was that it might explain why human women weren't always as receptive to amorous encounters as men were. My feelings were that this might have something to do with his ex wife. And maybe he had, after all, tried asking out that pretty East Indian woman, unsuccessfully. He was very often smiling, Chris, but he had a melancholy air as well. A far off look like he was reading a book even when he wasn't, even when he was operating the whirling, water-jetting, steam-billowing washer machine. I wanted to reach out to him, help him in some way, but I'm a man and we often find that hard and I didn't know what to say, what encouragement to give or comfort to offer.

On the following night I was reading Nabokov's "Lolita" at a cafeteria table by myself, waiting for Chris to come and read Mishima's "The Sailor Who Fell From Grace With The Sea" at the other end of the table, but not really thinking much of his absence. When he finally arrived and sat down, however, his face was flushed and his whisper intense. I asked him what was up and he told me.

He had been heading for the stairs, so as to go down to the locker room and retrieve his book, when he had passed a closet in the hall near the restrooms on the third floor, where we worked. Just as he reached the head of the stairs, he had heard a mumbled voice behind him. Turning, he imagined it was from the closed ladies' room. But as the indistinct voice trailed off, he had the impression it had come from the locked utility closet instead.

I suggested he was over-tired, as we all were constantly on the graveyard shift. Or it must have been someone in the ladies' room after all. But Chris got very defensive. Hey, he said, you guys are the ones who told me all those ghost stories. I know what I heard.

Well, you never know, I conceded. And I asked him what the voice had sounded like.

A woman, he said.

*

Just as on the outside EastCoast looks like it could be a futuristic colony on another planet, on the inside it reminds me of a hospital combined with a space station combined with a sweatshop. The glossy two-toned halls smell of disinfectant, the vast production rooms of isopropyl alcohol. Floors are either pristine or sticky with spilled medicine. As I mentioned, steam hisses out of machines, water pools on the floor, broken glass can be everywhere, cuts from such glass and burns from hot metal or scalding water are common. But there are also computers and banks of prettily lit buttons all about, so that the production bays have an odd blend of factory and high tech, old and new processes at work in noisy conjunction. The constant clack and jangle of glass fills the air. Glass bottles and ampoules move along conveyor belts in processions like marching, faceless soldiers . . . clear glass like drifts of shattered ice, amber glass vials that look like root beer candy you could suck on. Some of the workers, temps mostly, in blue uniforms, with most of us entirely in white like an army of apparitions who have been labouring here for generations in an endless loop of ghostly single-mindedness.

Zombies might be a better analogy. Third shift is a real challenge; the best thing to do is stick to a consistent sleep routine, but that's hard to accomplish. We shuffle about blurry-minded, and some of us like Daniel have bloodshot eyes that would make a zombie envious (then again Daniel works five hours of overtime a day, most the time). It's no wonder some of us hear things, see things out of the corner of our eyes. I've caught myself trying to use my credit card style ID tag, which serves both as my time card and unlocks doors within the plant, to gain access to my apartment when I get home. You might very well wonder by now if I've ever had a ghostly encounter myself. Nothing really to speak of, unless you count looking at my face in the mirror when I get home in the morning.

Maybe Chris was having an especially difficult time adjusting to third shift, though he didn't doze off in his chair in the plant or in the cafeteria like some did. Still, it wasn't long before he was looking extra pale, extra distant. We talked about books less. Since finishing "Lolita", I had moved on to its precursor "The Enchanter", but I noticed that Chris was reading one called "Phone Calls From The Dead", apparently penned by two parapsychologists. When I asked him about it, he seemed embarrassed and reticent as if afraid I'd make fun of him. But he said how there were many cases of ghosts communicating over phone lines. I told him it sounded fascinating and that he should show it to the solution prep people who had been getting those enigmatic phone calls on Friday nights.

Maybe my interest in the book renewed Chris's trust in me. Setting down the paperback, he leaned across the table toward me and related a new experience he had had in the plant several days prior.

I could see Chris had to hesitate, question his decision, before he proceeded with his story . . . but he told it nonetheless.

He had been walking down one of the many labyrinthine corridors of this glossy modern biotech company, on his way to dropping off some samples from our latest batch outside the microbiological lab for testing. And when he had deposited the samples and turned back into the hall, he had seen a woman disappear around a corner in the hallway ahead of him. The woman, he told me, was rather exotic looking, her skin dusky, with long black hair that looked matted and wet. And she didn't have a stitch of clothing on.

I know it was a mistake, but I couldn't help but laugh. Who could blame me? I teased Chris that it was a wishful hallucination. Maybe Chris was day-dreaming about Lee too much. A bit testily, he said the woman hadn't looked like Lee. Well, I asked him, did you follow her? And he told me that after a startled and faltering moment or two, he had indeed run forward and looked down that bend in the corridor. But the naked woman was not in sight.

I then asked if she had made eye contact with him. No, he told me. I teased him that next time he had better run faster, and get her phone number.

*

I didn't share either of Chris's strange encounters with the others, for fear that they would tease him even more than I had . . . would refer to the nude woman as a wet dream when he described the beads of water he had thought he saw glistening on her bare shoulders . . . would joke that if it were an employee who had taken a shower in the downstairs locker rooms, then she had gone a long way in search of a towel. I knew Chris was too sensitive a person to have to endure that kind of ridicule, however good-natured and playful it was bound to be. Still, maybe he should have shared his experiences with all of us. We were all open-minded about such things. Ama had many an eerie tale to relate from when she'd grown up in Ghana, and Ufuk had once told me a story some old Turkish relative had once told her about a woman who could turn into a cat (or was it the other way around?). Maybe then Chris might have told us about other sightings I suspected he witnessed, but didn't share . . . except for a final one that he reluctantly confided to me alone. He more or less had to, because I was with him at the time it occurred.

We had left together for our 4:30 AM second break, our respective books in hand, when Chris suddenly lagged behind me . . . turning so abruptly that his sneaker squealed on the polished corridor floor. Turning also, I saw him approach a closed office door with a window in it. The office was dark, and I saw Chris rattle the knob. It was locked.

Coming to his side as he stood there with his nose practically pressed to the glass, I asked him what he'd seen. After several beats of hesitance, Chris told me. While we had been walking, he'd peripherally glimpsed a figure in the door's window. And when he'd faced it, he'd recognised that same woman he had seen before. Naked, dusky, her hair plastered to her neck and the sides of her broad, pretty face. And this time, he told me, she was making direct eye contact with him.

I wanted to joke, "Does she have a sister?", but I refrained. Indulging him, in a thoughtful tone I suggested that Chris was more sensitive to these kinds of occurrences than the rest of us were. He only grunted distractedly, and finally, after seemingly peering into every shadowy corner of that office, peeled himself away from the glass.

*

Perhaps it was our fault. We all got Chris worked up about the supposed hauntings inside EastCoast Pharmaceuticals, by sharing our stories like campfire tales of old in that high-ceilinged cafeteria with its triangular fountain pool. We churned up each other's imaginations like silt on a lake bottom, heightened each other's fears and excitement, and made ourselves more susceptible to illusion and misinterpretation. We didn't realise that perhaps Chris was even more impressionable than the rest of us, that with him our talk might be some kind of catalyst.

I didn't personally witness any of the last events myself, but I pieced them together later with the help of my co-workers, as we huddled around one of the tables in the cafeteria.

Ama was the one who saw Chris take the key ring off the wall of Hassan's office, Hassan being our boss, on a night when Hassan had called in sick. This in itself wasn't too unusual, in that we used the various keys to unlock the metal cabinet where the big jugs of alcohol were stored, or the cages where we stored the wagons laden with filled product until they could be inspected by the interchangeable and generally disagreeable old Polish and Greek ladies on day shift.

It was Frederick who saw Chris in the hallway outside our production bays, near the restrooms at the head of the stairs. Frederick was going into the men's room, and thought it was a little odd that Chris would be unlocking the door to the utility closet a short distance away.

Since Chris was my partner on the cartridge washer, I was the one who noticed his absence first. Not wanting to get him in trouble, I asked my co-workers if they'd seen him before going to my group leader Patty about it, though I did ultimately do that. She in turn went to Hassan, who in turn ended up going to security. Ultimately, security called the police.

But before I went to Patty, I asked Frederick, and he told me about Chris unlocking that closet where Chris had told me he had heard a mumbling voice that time.

The closet was found to be locked, but another set of keys was quickly produced. Inside, security discovered Hassan's set of keys on the floor. But Chris was not there.

I myself, as I've said earlier, have never had an unexplained encounter inside EastCoast Pharmaceuticals, as I never did at Rosen

Thermographers. But every so often a new story is added to the lore we exchange at the cafeteria table.

And it wasn't so long ago that one of the women in solution prep told the rest of us that on a Friday night, third shift, when the plant is practically empty, she'd picked up a phone call and there hadn't been any voice on the other end. She was just about to hang up, when at last she thought she detected a few faraway, half indistinct words distorted by a hiss of static.

Though she hadn't known the new guy very well, she told us, the voice had sounded like Chris.

# SUSTAINING CHAOS:
# AN INTERVIEW WITH BRIAN STABLEFORD

## BY NICK GEVERS

INTRODUCTION

Brian Stableford, born in 1948, may well be the most persuasive, the most eloquent, contemporary British writer of SF and dark fantasy. Since early in his career, he has produced a stream of ingenious and subversive novels, which, whether space-operatic entertainments or extravagantly experimental metaphysical romances, have argued the case for transformation: radical transformation of the physical body through miracles of genetic engineering, and intellectual transformation through visionary contemplation and cogent polemical discussion. His books typify the Scientific Romance form his literary criticism has done so much to define: dark, cool, curious, and discursive, they dramatise and question the nature and application of Knowledge, exploring the long evolutionary perspectives bequeathed to British speculative fiction by Olaf Stapledon in a spirit of sarcastically provocative inquiry.

Stableford's early works, such as the *Dies Irae* trilogy (1971), were inventive but relatively lightweight; his distinctive brand of relentless biological speculation began to achieve full expression in the space operas of the *Hooded Swan* sequence (6 volumes, 1972-5) and the *Daedalus Mission* series (6 volumes, 1976-9). The most impressive and experimental works of the first phase of his career were the major novels *Man in a Cage* (1975), *The Mind-Riders* (1976), *The Realms of Tartarus* (1977), and *The Walking Shadow* (1979).

After some years in which he worked chiefly as an academic and critic, Stableford returned to fiction with tremendous vigour in 1988, with a voluminous revisionist vampire novel, *The Empire of Fear*. Its formidable rhetoric and atmospheric intensity carried over in full measure to Stableford's dark-fantastic masterpiece, the secret-historical trilogy made up of *The Werewolves of London* (1990), *The Angel of Pain* (1991), and *The Carnival of Destruction* (1994), as well as to the excellent stories in *Sexual Chemistry* (1991), the contemporary horror novel *Young Blood* (1992), and the superb Dracula-meets-H. G. Wells novella *The Hunger and Ecstasy of Vampires* (1996). More in the vein of his early sequences, the trilogy *The Books of Genesys* (1995-7) details the zoological splendours and mysteries of a far-off world, superficially in the manner of fantasy; a notable millennial comedy of the supernatural, *Year Zero*, appeared from the British independent publisher Sarob Press in 2000.

Just complete is a large and complex future history, first delineated in short stories from the mid-1980s on, and now developed in full: the "emortality" sequence, composed of *Inherit the Earth* (1998), *Architects of Emortality* (1999), *The Fountains of Youth* (2000), *The Cassandra Complex* (2001), *Dark Ararat* (2002), and *The Omega Expedition* (2002). Witty and argumentative, a conceptually vertiginous survey of humanity's future evolution couched in plots and language of elegant sarcasm, this sequence ranks amongst the great achievements of contemporary SF.

I interviewed Brian Stableford by e-mail in October 2002.

THE INTERVIEW

**NG:** You've published across a wide variety of speculative genres over the last thirty years, and much of your finest work is dark fantasy or horror. How would you sum up the current state of the horror/dark fantasy field, aesthetically and commercially?

**BS:** Commercially, it's very marginal. Although there are several high profile "brand name" writers who operate in the field there aren't enough readers who take an eclectic interest in the entire genre to justify the big publishers maintaining regular programmes. That's partly because the aesthetics of horror is an acquired taste, even in its broadest sense; most readers prefer comforting books where everything is guaranteed to come out right in the end. If you look more closely at the anatomy of the genre further issues arise, because there are various subspecies of "dark fantasy" whose aesthetics are very peculiar indeed—which is exactly what makes them interesting to their writers. What Lovecraft called "cosmic horror", the slightly surreal fiction of existential unease, and so on, are gourmet dishes that will never command a vast audience, but they offer particularly piquant delights to their connoisseurs.

**NG:** As perhaps the best read of all the historians and critics of speculative fiction: what do you see as the most important thematic components of macabre literature down the years? Which authors stand out as its most eminent and influential practitioners?

**BS:** I fear that my reputation for having read more imaginative fiction than almost anyone else can only go downhill now that my eyesight has deteriorated to the point where reading is becoming a chore. I'm more acutely conscious now than ever before of all the books I haven't read, because I know that I'm never going to be able to read all the ones currently in my possession, let alone any significant fraction of the rest.

As I've become more interested in the history and evolution of imaginative fiction my attention has become increasingly fixated on the 19th century, so it's easy enough to identify the writers who made ground-breaking contributions then. Poe and Hoffmann were the great pioneers of modern macabre fiction, who inspired dozens of followers. They were the first people to play extensively and variously with the grey area where objective and subjective experience overlap and become confused, and their understanding of the fragility of phenomenal reality—the construct in our heads which tries to represent things "as they are" but is always subject to the limitations of our senses and the perversities of our minds—provides the basic theme on which millions of variations have since been played out.

Twentieth century horror and dark fantasies have become so diverse that people with slightly different tastes are likely to come up with quite distinct accounts of who the "most important" writers are. I'm very fond of the writers constituting the Decadent Movements, so I find minor writers like Vernon Lee and M. P. Shiel more interesting than even the most obviously-influential ghost story writers, like M. R. James, but that's a personal idiosyncrasy. I love Clark Ashton Smith's work, but he's an essentially esoteric writer. Stephen King and Clive Barker are obviously entitled to be considered highly eminent and influential, but the obligation to please a wide audience and maintain best-seller status inevitably exerts pressure to avoid being "too difficult", and it seems to me that it's in the "difficult" bits that the most productive aesthetic hard labour is often done.

**NG:** Much horror/dark fantasy is metafictional or allusive in nature, overtly reworking earlier texts and traditions within the form. Why is this? Is modern horror necessarily postmodern, a self-referential literary and cinematic form?

**BS:** It's an inevitable consequence of the accumulation of texts. The extent of potential novelty is defined by what's already been done, and although the spectrum as a whole expands as time goes by, many of its subsidiary bands get used up (or at least clogged up). All "new" fiction is written and read in a context defined by an awareness of what has gone before, and the more detailed that awareness becomes the more it will bear directly on what gets written in the future. In addition, history—including literary history—is something that routinely gets re-examined and re-processed to take aboard the rewards of hindsight, so it's entirely natural that we should be interested in responding repeatedly to the significant texts of the past as our perception of their meaning and significance changes. The argument applies to all kinds of fiction (and, indeed, non-fiction), but the phenomenon is most obvious in those genres that are idea-centred rather than character-centred. Naturalistic fiction set in the present day can surf the wave of novelty served up in the daily newspapers, but imaginative fiction has by definition to reach out beyond the flow of everyday trivia, and its past achievements are inevitably more pervasive of its present endeavours.

**NG:** As you indicated earlier, you're an (extremely eloquent) champion of literary Decadence. Why is this? What makes the attitudes and techniques of Decadence so useful in the writing not only of horror and dark fantasy, but science fiction as well?

**BS:** I'm not sure how I acquired the psychological kink that makes me so sympathetic to the Decadent world-view and its associated literary methods. I've felt like an outsider for as long as I can remember, so I have no idea how that first developed, but I do recall deliberately refining a flamboyant cynicism and a cruelly-slanted sarcasm as a kind of survival strategy in secondary school. Any all-male adolescent institution is, inevitably, a highly competitive environment where "normality" involves everyone being as nasty as possible to everyone else at all times; being slightly-built and always looking several years younger than I actually was placed me at such a disadvantage physically that I overcompensated in other ways—and overcompensation isn't something one can do by halves. I've tried to tone it down over the years, but I guess the wind changed somewhere along the way and I got stuck with it.

The Decadent world-view is extremely useful in certain kinds of fantasy fiction because it's extremely detached, mercilessly sceptical and saturated with irony; it's very conducive to extrapolation in new directions—and also, of course, to new extremes. The conventional endings of most kinds of stories, which usually involve the restoration of a temporarily-lost normality or the acquisition of various stereotyped rewards, are grotesquely ill-fitted to dark fantasy and science fiction (although that doesn't stop moral imbeciles from trying to ram the square pegs into the round holes) and the Decadent world-view is a much better provider of appropriate closure in those genres.

**NG:** In your major works, you play elaborate games with your readers' expectations and perceptions: plots evaporate into inconsequentiality; most of the action can take place on the level of dreams; characters are preternaturally eloquent. Why so much sarcastic misdirection, convoluted oneirism, and polemical profligacy?

**BS:** Some people conceive of creativity as bringing order out of chaos, and some as bringing lumpiness out of uniformity. In fact, it's both; the basis of aesthetic experience is the constant flux of new harmonies arising out of previously inchoate elements, while those harmonies that have petrified into dogmas are blasted apart to renew the supply of raw materials. Readers being what they are (which makes editors what they are, poor things), there's always more demand for texts that celebrate the harmonizing part of the process, working towards order, contentment, self-satisfaction, etc. It is, however, logically necessary that a few bold souls should take on the opposite burden of creating and sustaining the awareness of chaos that generates the demand for orderers and flatterers. I hurt so badly when I hear someone saying that something is obvious that I just can't help suggesting that it not only isn't obvious but is very likely false; some people might regard that as a character flaw, but I prefer to think of it as a valuable public service.

On the other hand, maybe that's just so much pseudo-intellectual crap. Maybe it's just that, to me, people hitting one another—or hitting on one another—is essentially boring, while literary dreams are a fount of fabulous flexible fascination. I never have been able to figure out why most people feel differently.

**NG:** Drawing various themes together: your characteristic strategy is to ally genres in a devious way: a horror novel or a fantasy epic turns out to be science fiction; a science fiction novel expresses the logic of fantasy; Wellsian time travellers set out into the far future, and encounter vampires there. Why is this deft shuffling of genre masks so central to your oeuvre?

**BS:** All of my work is "science fiction" in the sense that it looks for explanations, and one kind of project that I've always been interested in is trying to construct worlds-within-texts which could actually support the kinds of entities which have featured prominently in fantasy fiction despite being flagrantly nonsensical, and hence utterly unbelievable: vampires, ghosts, prophecy, God, etc, etc. (I take it for granted, of course, that religion is merely fantasy fiction of a kind so blatantly inept that it has to substitute faith for the rational suspension of judgment.) I don't really think of my work as "shuffling genre masks", although I can see how it might look that way; I think of it as an attempt to catch a few glimpses, however fugitive, of what might lie behind the masks.

Another factor which might need to be taken into account with respect to this point is that I've never been one of nature's specialists. I tend more towards the end of the intellectual spectrum occupied by the people who know next-to-nothing about everything than the end occupied by people who know everything about next-to-nothing. Continually switching between different literary genres—not to mention between fiction, non-fiction, literary translation and teaching—helps me to stay busy without getting jaded. Sometimes, a change really is as good as a rest.

**NG:** Your breakthrough 1988 novel, *The Empire of Fear*, could be described as horror in the service of science fiction: vampires dominate the world during an alternate Renaissance, and must be understood scientifically before humanity can be liberated. Strong echoes of this approach sound in *Young Blood* and *The Hunger and Ecstasy of Vampires* (and of course, the still unpublished *The Gateway of Eternity*). Why is the vampire for you such a powerful symbol both (as traditionally) of carnal and religious elements and (untraditionally) of the potential for scientific revelation?

**BS:** In the 1980s I became very interested in "revisionist" vampire fiction, which hauled the motif out of the frame of Victorian neurosis—where it tended to embody anxieties about sex—and built a new one, in which its sexual connotations were accommodated to modern erotic sensibility. I was also fascinated by the use of the vampire as a hypothetical entity in the construction of an alternative "existential predicament", with its own highly distinctive *angst*. The three projects you mention (*The Hunger and Ecstasy of Vampires* expanded into *The Gateway of Eternity*, of which it remains an element) were alternative ways of trying to accommodate vampires within a rational world-view, track the possible implications of their existence, and suggest the appropriate intellectual attitudes that might be taken towards them. I was, of course, standing on the shoulders of giants: Pierre Kast, Fred Saberhagen, Chelsea Quinn Yarbro and Suzy McKee Charnas, to name but a few.

That interest in the evolution of the idea of the vampire became a key component of my interest in excavating forgotten tracts of literary history (particularly French literary history). It also resulted in my becoming fascinated by the temporary adoption of vampiric imagery into Gothic rock music and lifestyle fantasy. We little know when first we mount our hobby-horses how far they might take us into strange and wonderful territories.

**NG:** Your *Werewolves of London* trilogy is an extraordinary experiment: dreams, gods, visits to Heaven and Hell, hauntings, fell transformations, alternate histories all are not as they seem; and intellectual debate rages over hundreds of pages. What was the creative evolution of this huge tapestry? Does its final form achieve all you'd intended, and is it indeed your magnum opus?

**BS:** For various reasons unconnected with its ultimate sales to the public, *The Empire of Fear* made a lot of money before publication, enthusing the editor who had commissioned it to the extent that she was absolutely avid to sign up something else. I'd only given her the outline for *The Empire of Fear* as a second-string in case she didn't want to do *Les Fleurs du Mal* (which eventually appeared 13 years later, after a very chequered history, as *Architects of Emortality*) and she still didn't want to do that one, so I mentioned that I'd been toying with the idea of a fantasy in which a peculiar alloy of mythical and actual history would be observed by an immortal werewolf. The last two words clinched the deal, but when I submitted the outline for a 200,000-word book she asked me to redesign it as two somewhat-more-economical volumes (she'd already made me cut the text of *The Empire of Fear* from 200,000 words to 180,000). Rejigging the material forced me to abandon the chronological sequence I'd originally planned; I enclosed the earlier parts of the history within the main, 19th-century, narrative and moved the werewolf, Pelorus, from centre-stage to the wings. When I put the new outline in, the editor said: "You couldn't make it a trilogy, could you? They sell *so* well." So I did what I could to manufacture a second sub-climax . . .

By the time I actually delivered *Werewolves*, alas, the commissioning editor was long gone and the whole publishing industry had gone from boom to bust. The publication process was fouled up by sadly unsuccessful attempts to minimise losses, and it looked for a while as if I wouldn't be able to complete the project at all. It ended up far more of a patchwork than I'd originally intended, with a much more convoluted structure, but that's not entirely to its disadvantage. I still think very fondly of some of its bits, although there are other bits that don't really fit and are there for the wrong reasons.

I currently think of the six-volume emortality series as my "magnum opus", but I hope to write another ten million words before I die, so there may yet be an opportunity to supersede it.

**NG:** In the mid-Nineties, you wrote *Genesys*, a big planetary romance fantasy trilogy, with hard-scientific biological speculation as its true rationale. In such science fantasy, how readily can fantasy and SF be made to work in synergy? Are their contradictions fertile creative ground?

**BS:** "Fantasy" is a broad and somewhat discontinuous spectrum. I pitched *Genesys* to various editors as an SF novel that would look like a genre fantasy trilogy, hoping that at least one of them would think it a neat marketing gimmick. In retrospect, it might not have been a good move—the money it lost its publishers practically guaranteed that I would never sell anything in the UK again, but I might have got into that position whatever else I'd done instead.

Formulaic quest fantasy is, in fact, completely incompatible with science fiction, because it has a built-in requirement for exactly the kind of quick-fix feelgood endings that morally responsible SF cannot accommodate. I suppose it was inevitable that my chimerical hybrid would end up falling between the two stools and appealing to no one, but it seemed like a good idea at the time.

Other kinds of fantasy—including dark fantasy—can be much more profitably alloyed with SF, and often are. If there's a synergistic effect to be found anywhere it's in the kind of territory I tried to explore (with a similar dismal lack of commercial success) in *Young Blood* and *Year Zero*, using a manifest clash of explanatory schemes to heighten the disturbing quality of extraordinary events. *Year Zero* is a comedy as well as a melodrama, and the stark clash of the explanations advanced within the text helped me to generate the humour as well as complicating the mystery element. *Kiss the Goat: A Twenty-First Century Ghost Story*, which should be forthcoming from Prime Press in the early months of 2003, is yet another venture into that ambiguous territory, and I shall probably return to it at frequent intervals in spite of the lack of financial encouragement. I think these three novels are among my best, and I must confess that I can't really understand why the work I've done in this vein has had such a hard time in the commercial marketplace—the work in question seems to me to be far more accessible to the ordinary reader than *The Empire of Fear* and *Werewolves of London*, even though the endings of the stories sometimes require a certain leap of the imagination to be fully appreciated.

**NG:** Many of your short stories are sardonic fairy tales. How do you define the cultural function of the fairy tale, and why do you twist it so about?

**BS:** Even in a complex society like ours standardized folktales provide a set of cultural references that everyone can relate to, because we all encounter them as young children and then assist in their transmission to our own children. They provide a neutral territory in which adults and children can meet and communicate as equals, because everybody knows the same things about them and there's nothing else to know. That gives them a unique utility as transformable templates, and as anchorages for new imaginative departures. The most common ones tend to have survived so long, and spread so widely, because they echo anxieties and frustrations that many children experience as they grow up, and which many adults never entirely outgrow; that makes them perpetually ripe for reinterrogation, reanalysis, further extrapolation and continual challenge—which is what "twisting them about" amounts to.

**NG:** Now that your big "emortality" SF series for Tor is complete, what lies next for you? Any further dark decadent fantasies, or steampunk epics?

**BS:** I recently submitted *The Curse of the Coral Bride*, the first volume of a new projected six-volume series, to Tor, but haven't yet had a response. It's a series of far-futuristic fantasies which will attempt to do for the Zothique/Dying Earth scenario what *The Empire of Fear* did for vampires and *The Werewolves of London* for gods, etc—i.e. construct a world-within-the-texts in which that fabulously exotic imaginative apparatus becomes rationally plausible, and then examine some of the questions arising in consequence. We know that we're here, and that we won't be here for long, because that's the way the evolutionary cookie has so far crumbled—but in a few billion years' time, when countless posthuman species have come and gone, the last mortal inhabitants of the doomed world might have to find very different explanations for why they've been abandoned to vulgar mortality and imminent extinction, and cursed with workable magic. In volume six, when the world will actually end, the final answers will be delivered—unless, of course, nobody wants to publish the books (my by-line is now sufficient reason for the rejection of any book in the UK, and Tor seems to represent the Last Chance Saloon so far as the US market is concerned, so it's entirely possible that nobody will).

If the new series does sell, at the standard rate of a book a year, I'll fill in the gaps in my schedule with the usual mix of quirky stand-alone novels, short fiction, reference-book hackwork and translations of obscure French fiction. If not, I'll have to think hard about a Plan B. The "career" of my *alter ego* Brian Craig is also in limbo at present, while the loremasters at Games Workshop decide whether he is worth the kind of money and the degree of creative latitude he is currently asking for. If they decide to dispense with his services, I'll probably need to come up with a Plan C as well, and maybe a Plan D. Fortunately, the quarter of me that still has an honest job—teaching on an M.A. course in "Writing for Children" at King Alfred's College, Winchester—has avoided the most recent round of staff redundancies (presumably the authorities thought that it wasn't worth the bother of saving a quarter salary when the objective was to save a few whole ones) and may yet evolve into the principal breadwinner of our curious collective.

www.ingramcontent.com/pod-product-compliance
Lightning Source LLC
Chambersburg PA
CBHW031257060726
47590CB00003B/948